CHADRON STATE COLLEGE
5086 00390813

P9-DGG-108

ORFE

BOOKS BY CYNTHIA VOIGT

Homecoming

Dicey's Song

Winner of the 1983 Newbery Medal

A Solitary Blue

1984 Newbery Honor Book

Tell Me If the Lovers Are Losers

The Callender Papers

Winner of the 1984 Edgar Allan Poe Award

Building Blocks

The Runner

Jackaroo

Izzy, Willy-Nilly

Come a Stranger

Stories about Rosie

Sons from Afar

Tree by Leaf

Seventeen against the Dealer

On Fortune's Wheel

The Vandemark Mummy

Orfe

CYNTHIA VOIGT

Atheneum • 1992 • New York

Maxwell Macmillan Canada
Toronto
Maxwell Macmillan International
New York Oxford Singapore Sydney

Atheneum
Macmillan Publishing Company
866 Third Avenue
New York, NY 10022

Maxwell Macmillan Canada, Inc.
1200 Eglinton Avenue East
Suite 200
Don Mills, Ontario M3C 3N1

Macmillan Publishing Company is part of the Maxwell Communication Group of Companies.

First edition

Printed in the United States of America

10 9 8 7 6 5 4 3 2 1

Book design by Patrice Fodero

Library of Congress Cataloging-in-Publication Data

Voigt, Cynthia.
Orfe / Cynthia Voigt.
p. cm.
Summary: Enny tells of her relationship with Orfe, an unusually talented musician, and of the love between Orfe and Yuri, a recovering addict.
ISBN 0-689-31771-9
[1. Rock music—Fiction. 2. Drug abuse—Fiction.] I. Title.
PZ7.V874Or 1992
[Fic]—dc20 91-46058

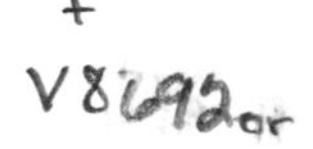

For Walter,

because it's a love story

ONE

This is what I remember:

I am sitting at a school desk. A wooden desk top with an open shelf of ridged blue pipe metal under it, the desk stands on spindly piped-metal legs. I am sitting on a chair made out of wood and metal. It is recess and we're inside, so it must be raining.

The new girl is assigned the desk next to mine, on my left. On my right is a chalkboard, all along the wall. The desk next to mine is the only empty desk in the classroom and it is empty because—why do I remember this so clearly?—Heather's father had been transferred to Fort Pendleton, so Shirl, who from the beginning of the year had sat next to me, had asked if she could switch into Heather's old desk, next to Frannie. Frannie is the Queen of the class; so when Frannie asked Shirl to ask the teacher if she could move, and Shirl wanted to, I didn't blame her, even though it left me alone next to an empty desk. I'd have done the same.

The new girl is assigned to what used to be Shirl's desk, next to mine.

The new girl has red hair, carroty red, in wiry curls. She's short and scrawny and pale. She wears jeans, shirt, sneakers, gold hoop earrings in pierced ears. She isn't looking around, she doesn't expect anyone to talk to her, she doesn't expect to talk to anyone, she doesn't care.

I do care, which is why I am coloring a gown for a paper doll. Frannie announced a contest, to draw the best outfits for your paper doll. I have my box of forty-eight Crayola crayons—copper, silver, and gold included—open at my right hand. I have a brunette paper doll in a red bathing suit and red high-heeled shoes beside the box of crayons; I trace her outline onto my paper. I am bored of paper dolls after about five minutes, and bored with designing outfits after about two minutes, and I keep the gown simple. I draw a long dress, floor-length to cover the red shoes, long-sleeved and high-necked. I color it dark blue. When you are making outfits for a paper doll, you have to make a gown and a pair of pajamas and a sports outfit—usually shorts, although it can be winter and you can do a ski outfit or a skating outfit. And you have to make a day dress or skirt and sweater. Once you've done those you can quit if you want to.

I finish coloring the long skirt. I think the new girl must be admiring me out of the corner of her eye. Everybody says Frannie is the best drawer in the class, but I think I am, although I would never say so. I am humming a song everybody is singing, one which the boys have declared cool, in the smirking way that tells me the lyrics have something to do with sex. I am smart enough to know I don't understand that part of it, although I pretend I do; but it seems to me that I do understand the other part, the sadness part of it. I hum softly, her hand gestures, she reaches over to the paper. I smile and nod, take out another sheet, and start to draw a maze.

That year I draw mazes whenever I can, square mazes, rectangular mazes, circular, triangular, trapezoidal, rhomboid, ovoid. I draw them for the pleasure of their intricate pathways and the one secret route into the heart. I draw them for the pleasure of the controlling shape that governs whatever space the mazes occupy.

The new girl reaches over and takes the copper crayon out of my box. She begins to color on my drawing of the gown. I think she shouldn't be doing that, but I don't know how to stop her. She is humming a song I don't know, quietly, as she colors. Her face is hidden by the long wiry hair. Whatever she is doing to my drawing is hidden by the curve of her hand and arm.

I go back to the maze, working outward from its heart.

When the new girl returns my paper to me, she doesn't wait for my reaction.

My reaction is surprise. What is bad about the gown is that it isn't fancy enough, but she hasn't fixed that, with flounces or lace or belt. She has made wings, huge wings, that spread out behind the shoulders in great floating copper arcs. I had never thought angel wings might be copper. "It's not an angel," I say to her.

"It isn't?"

She takes the paper back and looks at it.

"Yes it is," she says. "Can't you see it?"

And I can see that it might be.

When I have spread my lunch out on the top of the desk—sandwich and fruit, square container of milk, four Oreo cookies wrapped in waxed paper—they come circling around, five of them, or four, or six. Their noses jab down at me. "One way to find out what a prisoner knows," says Robby or Rip, "is you don't ever let him fall asleep. Day after day. If he falls asleep, you wake him up, by sticking knives into him, or electric shocks, cold water—you can make him stay awake."

"That breaks him down," adds Robert or Rupert.

"A few days," says Rab or Bobby. "A few days of that and then they pull him out of his cell—the cells have no light, no windows, not even a crack, it's as black as a coffin inside. His eyes are red, and he's trembling, the shakes, probably looks like an addict, or a drunk with d.t.'s. Wanna bet?"

"I bet. I bet. Scared shitless."

"Begging them to let him sleep. Begging to tell them anything they want to know."

"Begging for help, but there's nobody there to help, nobody can help him."

What is the same about them is their voices, the way they start speaking the cruelty and have no power to stop themselves. Cruelty urges or calls them onward, and they dive more deeply into it, as if they could get drunk on cruelty, addicted to violence, swallowed up and besotted, as if they heard their own voices speaking the words and fell in love with the sounds of violence in their own voices.

" 'D'joo see about that girl, in the mud slide, in Brazil? Enny, did you see that? How nobody could get to her, so she was just stuck there? They took pictures, while she was dying. She was our age."

"It took days, didn't it?"

"Only her head was out in the air."

"The rest of her—"

"I guess the other people got out of the village in time."

"Wasn't this in Mexico? Or was there another one in Mexico too?"

"I guess she was just too slow a runner. But mud slides move fast, there's not much chance, a lot of the people in her village just got—"

I study my sandwich—bologna and yellow mustard on white bread, without any butter—but I have to hear. I don't cover my ears. I have to listen, until I am gulping, and tears plop down onto the desk and onto the top of my sandwich, and then they go away.

My hands are cramped on top of my desk. I move them to my lap. When I look over, the new girl sits with her head bent, her face hidden.

Her name was Orfe and she was everything I wasn't. She was my best friend.

That first day, when she finished her lunch, she jammed crumpled-up waxed paper into the brown bag and said, "I can throw up whenever I want to."

She seemed to expect some response. I had wiped my eyes, but my nose was still stuffy; I had no response to make.

"There are things, if I think them and picture them? I can make myself throw up. It's called projectile vomiting." She demonstrated, her hand raised to her mouth with fingers curled, then flung open, outward. "I can projectile vomit when I want to, Enny." She bent her head then, and her face was hidden again.

This was a mannerism, I learned. Orfe would bow her head and her eyes would fill up with what she was feeling so that when she raised her face—if she raised her face, that is, because sometimes she kept it hidden—whatever she was feeling was loosed, full force, out of her eyes.

When she did that, it was impossible to misunderstand Orfe. When she raised her face and loosed her glance, what she meant was clearer than words spoken aloud.

The Creature from Outer Space is what Frannie called her. Orfe didn't seem to mind, but I didn't want Orfe to be left out. I wanted her to be happy, so I made protests. "You should ask Orfe to your sleepover," I suggested to Frannie.

"The Creature from Outer Space? Why, did she ask you to ask me?"

"I just think it's mean to leave her out."

"No it's not," Frannie said, and giggled at her own

wit. "So I guess if you don't go anywhere the Creature isn't going, then she's your best friend now."

"I didn't say that," I denied, and was so ashamed of myself that I hated Frannie and was afraid of her. "I think you're being mean."

"Just because you think so doesn't make it true. So you can go back and tell your new best friend *that*. There's nothing either one of you can do about it anyway. It's *my* sleepover."

I even went so far as to offer Orfe my boyfriend. "You can have Leo," I told her, "for your boyfriend." I didn't bother saying that Leo wasn't much. She had to know that.

"Dumb." Orfe's voice came out from behind a tangle of hanging hair.

She was right. It was a dumb idea. And he was dumb, I was dumb, the whole setup was dumb, and Orfe was right not to want to take any part in it.

We explored the nearby patches of woods, wandering along by streams, and we talked. We explored the streets of the town, and we talked. We jumped rope, rode bikes, played cards, and we talked. To talk was to discover differences.

"It's the most . . . the best . . . story. Ever," I would say.

"But, Enny, you always say that about what you're reading, if you like it," Orfe pointed out.

"So what?"

"So nothing. It's just true."

"That's not so bad," I defended myself.

"I didn't say it was bad. Did I?"

"No," I admitted.

"It's the way you are, it's always what's right now with you. Never before or after, just now."

I knew what she meant, but I didn't want to talk about it. It was enough just to get through every day. "What about you?" I asked.

"I think about the future. Like, what I want to do, who I want to be."

"Really? What do you?"

"Famous," Orfe said.

She made me laugh sometimes, just laugh. "And rich?"

"I don't care about rich."

I believed her. "Famous for what?"

"Music."

"As a singer?" I guessed. "Even Frannie has to admit how good you are in singing."

But Orfe was shaking her head. "For my own songs, I want to write songs, and the music, and perform them. I want to sing so everyone hears me. I want . . ." She bent her head. "I want to write a song that's so true . . ." She raised her face and her eyes shone. "A song like fire, like ice."

"If anyone can do that, you can," I said as soon as I could catch my breath to speak, under the shining of her eyes. "Is it a rock star? Is that what you mean? Because if you got famous, you could hire me. Famous people need secretaries; I bet I'd be a good secretary. Or your housekeeper."

"I'd rather have you in the band."

"But I'm no good at music. I can't sing. I can't dance. I can't play anything."

"And you don't have much sense of rhythm, do you?" Orfe said. "So, but you could be the manager."

"What does a manager do?"

Orfe thought, then shrugged her shoulders to say she didn't know.

"I'd be good at being your secretary," I said. "Would you hire me?"

"As manager," Orfe said.

We played endless games of cribbage. I taught Orfe how to shuffle a deck of cards and then riff them together. We would decide how many times around the cribbage board our game would run and then deal out hand after hand, as we played out the run, leapfrogging our markers around the tracks.

"He was a frog, and that's slimy, cold," Orfe said. "I wouldn't want any frog sleeping on my pillow. Would you? I wouldn't want to have to let him share everything."

"If I make a promise, I ought to keep it," I said. "The princess shouldn't ever have promised if she didn't mean it."

"That was to get the ball back," Orfe explained.

"And she shouldn't have thrown him against the wall. Just—thrown him, like that." I could imagine how that would feel, to fly helpless through the air and slam into the wall. I wondered if you would feel your skin splitting and your bones being smashed. I wondered how it would feel to have someone hate you that much.

"But it's not about the frog, it's about the ball, the

way the ball is perfect. If I had a golden ball and it was perfect, I'd promise anything to get it back."

"It's about the frog. Or the prince, they're the same. Maybe it's about throwing him against the wall. He couldn't have turned into a prince unless she threw him against the wall."

"He couldn't have turned into a prince if it wasn't for the golden ball, Enny. The perfect thing."

"If you don't keep your promises, you aren't good enough to have the perfect thing, are you?" I asked.

"He had no right to make her promise," Orfe said.

"That doesn't matter, if you've promised. You have to keep it."

Orfe held her hands up, cupped, as if they held a golden ball in them. I could almost see it shining there in her hands. When it was shining there in her hands, I could see why you would promise anything to get it back if you lost it. Even if you didn't mean to keep your promise.

Orfe was always being different. Except for Friday afternoons after singing class when they forgot about that, everybody thought Orfe was the Creature from Outer Space, an alien being.

I couldn't exactly blame them. I didn't dare disagree with them, except by having Orfe for my friend; that was all I dared at the time. But the way Orfe would break rules, there were times I could see what everybody meant.

Like red rover. Red rover was the game we played at recesses that year. We would be picked into two teams, with Frannie as one captain and Rab as the other, and the rest of us waiting to be chosen for one team or the other. Hoping we wouldn't be left until last. Orfe was always the very last chosen. The rule was, of course, that everybody had to be on one team or on the other.

To start the game, one team joined hands and stretched out in a line across the macadam playground. The other team milled around facing the first team. Then the captain of the first team, firm at the center of his line, called out a name. Sometimes it was the fastest, strongest runner who was called first, the biggest threat selected when the line of defense was freshest, strongest. Sometimes it was the weakest runner.

If the runner broke through, that captain got to pick someone to change onto his team. If the runner failed to break through, it was the runner who had to change teams. Until someone broke through, the line held its position. When someone broke through, the teams switched sides, and what had been the line separated into individual team members, who became the milling group out of which a runner would be called.

It was a game of team spirit and individual achievement, of loyalty to your captain and hope for your own heroism. It was a game for standing fast and sturdy but also for running quick and clever. To be on Rab's team was better than to be on Frannie's, the King being better than the Queen; and in fact Rab's team most often won the game. But Orfe—

Orfe changed the rules, she wouldn't keep to the rules. She didn't care if her team won, if her captain was the winner. Everybody yelling at her at once couldn't make her do what they wanted. She broke the game down into chaos. Nobody ever knew, on any day, what Orfe would do, how she would play.

Orfe in the line sometimes, and never for any reason, let go of both the hands she held, to start turning in a circle with her fingers twined high over her head. Or sometimes she turned to grab both of a teammate's hands and raise them up to make a gate; the world shifted before the runner's eyes as if between the moment he was called and the moment he reached the line the game itself had been changed, from red rover to London Bridge.

Or if Orfe was called to run—and she ran fast, unexpectedly fast, effortlessly—she would dart toward one section, then feint to another side, run backward, or simply run down around the end of the long line, and the line would pull itself sideways like a drunken snake to try to keep Orfe in the game. Sometimes Orfe fell onto her knees to crawl underneath the wreathed arms, causing everyone to crouch down so that—sometimes—she would jump up then and jump over the barrier of bodies and arms, to run on, laughing. Or she might dance, singing, up and down the line—sing, dancing, back and forth—until in anger and laughter they would come to mill around her, her own team as well as the opponents, and follow her around the playground.

The geometry of line and moving dot that was red rover Orfe could at any time turn into chaos: Because where she sang, people gathered around her, and when she sang, the rules seemed impotent.

"Pain like you can't imagine," they said. "Imagine it."

"She can't *begin* to imagine."

That wasn't correct.

"Like putting cigarettes out on him. On his chest."

"His face—"

"The insides of his elbow—"

"They get excited. You know what I mean."

"They get off on it."

"Listening to him screaming, blubbering."

They had found me alone on the playground and circled around me.

"Nobody can do anything to make them stop."

"Like the river, the way nobody can stop chemicals being dumped in the river, poisoning the water, killing everything."

"A company is too big. Too powerful. It's got friends in government and nobody can stop government. It's too big."

"Yeah, if you're strong enough, nobody can ever stop you from what you're doing."

"Or if you've got weapons. Like nuclear bombs. Imagine a nuclear bomb."

The ends of my mouth pulled down and I couldn't stop the quivering. My eyes overflowed.

"It was just an ordinary morning," they said, "like today, and there must have been kids in school then too."

"And they blew everything up, all it took was planes in the sky, the *Enola Gay*."

The sky overhead was empty.

"Before you could turn your head to see what it was—whoosh—gone—"

"Except for the survivors. 'D'joo *see* those pictures, Enny?"

I had seen them.

"Except for the ones who looked normal, after, but there was radiation and they had monster babies—"

Orfe stood with her head bent down.

"It happens here too, but they don't tell you. It's in the air. From the testing. In milk because the cows eat the grass that grows in the air. Nobody can stop them. They're the government, they're the army."

Tears oozed down my cheeks. I was sick with fear and pity.

"If you're the strong one or rich or just big—like parents—"

"Nobody can stop parents from beating their kids."

"And the kids snivel, like Enny, or they'll scream if it's bad enough—"

"And the parents like that, a lot of them do. It's a turn-on. Know what I mean?"

"*She* wouldn't know. She doesn't know anything about anything."

Orfe raised her face to look at me. *What's wrong with you?* I could hear, as clear as if she'd said it.

I didn't know. I couldn't help it.

▲▲▲▲▲

"I really hate it when you cry like that," Orfe said.

My eyes filled with tears. I couldn't say anything, for fear of crying if I tried to say something.

"Look," Orfe said. "I didn't say you shouldn't cry. I said you shouldn't cry like that. When they start in on you, the way you sort of weep with your head bent like some . . . slave or something."

"I know. I'm sorry," I said, tears oozing out and mucus thickening in my nose and thickening my voice.

"Just letting them get away with it," Orfe said.

I nodded and wiped my nose with the back of my hand, then wiped my hand on the seat of my jeans.

"Helpless, I hate it when you—"

I shook my head, to clear it, to get her attention, to tell her she'd better stop saying that, please. "I can't help it," I explained.

"I know." Orfe's eyes filled with tears, but she blinked them clear. "I know. I know exactly. You have to *do* something to those boys."

"They'd just laugh. It wouldn't make any difference."

"Just because you're crying doesn't mean you can't hit someone—or throw something—your lunch box or your desk. That desk could hurt somebody. Or you could kick—kick Rab because they all do what he tells them to, that's what they're doing. You know what I mean?"

I knew what she meant.

"Or yell at them, at least. You can cry and still do all those things. It doesn't have anything to do with crying. I would too, I don't blame you."

"I do," I said. I turned to go home.

"Wait." Orfe's hand held my arm and she tried to pull me around.

"I'm sorry." I just wanted to get away and go home.

"For what?" Orfe asked.

I wished she'd leave me alone.

"Where are you going, Enny?"

"Home."

"Why?"

"Because—" But I couldn't say it. "Because—"

Orfe shook her red hair and lost patience with me. "You make me so mad, you really—"

"I *said* I was sorry."

"You act like you're nothing, some absolute nothing. You're as pretty as Frannie and you know it, even prettier in your own way. And better at math than anyone in the class. But you act as if, if you can't be one particular way, you're nothing. As if there was one way you had to be—"

I stared at Orfe, but she didn't notice me.

"It's so dumb and you're really smart." Her feet danced on the sidewalk in impatience and anger. "You're more like me than anyone I ever met before!"

"No, I'm not." I was shocked. "Orfe, I'm not at all like—I'm not musical at all. I care about school, I like school. I'm not brave. I care about other people, I pay attention, I'm not self-centered. I'm just *or*-di nary."

"It's ordinary to be self-centered," Orfe said to me. She was standing still now and about to burst out laughing—I could see that in her eyes. "Maybe you're the one who's extraordinary."

Orfe cared about having me for her friend. She cared

about me. Nothing much else mattered at that moment. "I feel better," I said, which was the truth.

But they still returned and circled me in the hallway or on the playground or at my desk. I still hunched down over my desk until I wept with their words.

Orfe at her desk next to mine had her own head bent—as I now understood—so that she wouldn't have to witness my shame.

Until one day she raised her face and it was anger shooting out of her eyes. "Cut that out," she said. "You, Rab—what you're saying is—horrible, you're—"

Rab's cheeks were pink and his eyes were bright. "Lookit that, will you?" he asked. " 'D'joo hear? The Creature speaks."

Orfe pushed herself up from her seat. "The things—what you're saying—"

I didn't know what she was going to do, I couldn't imagine.

They were laughing. Orfe was about halfway standing up, leaning toward Rab with her hands flat on the desk and her face pushing toward him—when she threw up. She vomited—it was sickening—hard, so hard that some of it spattered onto Rab's face from his chest. You could hear the vomit hitting his chest.

I stopped crying. I wiped at my eyes. I was worried about Orfe, if she was sick and how I could help.

Orfe vomited again, like a hand pump when the pressure comes right and suddenly water pumps out.

I remembered that she'd said she could do it on purpose. I sat dumb and wondered.

Rab tried to leap back, but the boys were in his way. "Goddamn it!" he bellowed.

Orfe leaned forward, turning her head to one side, like pointing a hose. The boys behind Rab scuttled away. "You fucking did that on fucking purpose!" Rab shouted in a fury, his chest dripping, chunks falling, and a stink rising from him.

Rab was of course sent home. The teacher dragged him out of the room by his arm for swearing like that. The principal suspended him for two days. I accompanied Orfe to the nurse's room and sat with her while she recovered. I had the foresight to bring my lunch box with me, and we shared the sandwich, cookies, and fruit equally between us.

▲▲▲▲▲

Orfe had routed them and I was proud of her, but the day Rab returned they were back, and Orfe was sitting with her head bent, and my eyes were filling with tears. It was as if all of Orfe's victory was good for nothing, except that they stood a safe distance back from her desk now. All the trouble she had gotten Rab into was worth only a few inches in the end. As if what Orfe did wasn't worth anything.

So I took my lunch box and tried to hit Rab in the face with it, or over the head. My lunch box was metal and had sharp corners. He grabbed it, but I wasn't about to let it go. I kept my hold on the handle even while I was pulled up out of my chair, and I came around from behind the desk—where I could kick at his shins while he held my lunch box over my head and danced his legs free. I don't know what he was saying because I was crying. But now I was crying from the sheer excitement of hitting at Rab and kicking him.

I had detention that day, copying over one hundred times, "I will not fight in school."

The next day I got a good clip in, across his cheek and nose, a wide broadhand with the lunch box, before he could block it. Blood poured out of his nose, and I spent the afternoon sitting on a chair out in the hallway. I sat alone, with nothing to do, no books or papers, feeling glad. Feeling as if I had been shut up in a little closet, but now I had broken down the walls and broken myself free.

After that, a couple of times, I was sent to the principal. I didn't care and it didn't make any difference to the way I acted. If Rab came near me and jabbed his nose at me that way, I would go crazy. Sometimes I would cry and go crazy, and sometimes I would not-cry and go crazy. But every time I would try to club him a good one—on the hands or head, ears or elbows, anywhere it would hurt. Rab had no idea what to expect, and his friends hung back, out of danger. Rab only kept at it because he was embarrassed not to. I would hit him with my fist or my lunch box, or I'd shove my desk right into his hips—except after the first time I did that, he was always ready to hop back, away.

After a while Rab just gave up; they all did. "Who wants to waste time fighting a girl," he muttered. They groused to themselves, "Girls are crybabies anyway, they don't fight fair, you're always never allowed to hurt them. Who cares?" they said.

Orfe raised her face at that and looked at me. I don't know what I looked like, with rage draining out of me, but Orfe's eyes shone out glad. *That's what I mean,* I could hear, as clear as if she said it. I think my eyes must have been shining too.

Even though I moved away and left Orfe behind, I didn't forget her. Even if I'd never seen her again, I would have remembered Orfe. As it was, I wasn't surprised to be the one she asked to go before them when she and Yuri walked out together to be married. I think my eyes must have been shining then too, and I know that Orfe and Yuri radiated a sense of loving that I can still warm my hands at, if I close my eyes and remember.

TWO

I don't remember why I was on that street on that day, at that time. I saw the gathering of people at the same time that I heard the singer's voice. The song floated like light. Both particle and wave, if light, the song seemed unlike anything else in the sensual world.

The singer stood with bent head, so I could see only a long mass of copper-colored curls. Then she raised her head in a remembered gesture and I recognized Orfe, across all the years.

In jeans, turtleneck, and boots, Orfe could have been taken for a scrawny young man or a slender young woman; it didn't matter which. Her hair spread around her face like a cloud. Her eyebrows were dark, and her narrow nose almost projected into a hook. When she had finished singing, hands went into pockets and purses to find money to drop into the upturned hat at Orfe's feet.

Until the crowd had disbanded, Orfe didn't notice

me. When she did, she picked up the hat without counting what was in it and came toward me.

I wasn't sure of her then. "Orfe?"

"Have I changed that much?"

I shook my head to say no. "Older."

"It's been years. What did you expect?"

I shook my head again, to clear my thoughts, for wonder. I had never expected anything and certainly not—

Orfe opened the hat and peered into it. "I can buy you a cup of coffee."

"More than one." I poked my finger at a ten-dollar bill.

"Unh-uh," Orfe said. "My room for the night comes out of this, and meals."

"Stay with me," I invited her. "It's a dormitory, but I've got a single, plenty of floor space."

She didn't hesitate to accept any more than I had hesitated to ask. "In that case, I can buy you a sandwich. Aren't you hungry? Don't tell me anything yet, wait until we sit down and I can really pay attention—and you, you too, you can really pay attention. Wait'll you hear what's been going on with me."

I couldn't imagine and, imagining, was already caught up in Orfe's excitement. But first I had to answer her questions about myself as we ate, and drank glass after glass of iced tea, and talked. "Why a degree in business?" Orfe asked.

Most people thought that but didn't ask. "I want to earn a good living. I'm good at management and applied economics, statistics, fitting all the pieces together." Most people thought that if you were a business major, you weren't their kind of person. "The workplace is so much of your life, you know? Work is so central, what you do to make your living."

"You don't look like a business major," Orfe said.

"What do I look like?"

"Who'd have thought you'd turn out so lovely?"

"Not me," I admitted. "But I'm glad I did. I enjoy it."

"Good for you." She studied me. "Not beautiful but—almost as if you are. People must look at you a second time and be disappointed."

I had forgotten Orfe's way of saying exactly what she thought, rather than what she thought you wanted to hear. I had forgotten what it felt like to have something nobody seemed to understand understood. "Yeah," I said, and felt the smile on my face. I couldn't stop smiling. "It's enough to make a person insecure, if she's banking on her looks. But you too, you've turned out—" I stopped, because she wasn't pretty, wasn't even fine-looking, was only just barely not unattractive; except of course that there was something about Orfe that made you want to look at her and keep on looking. Arresting.

"I wear myself naked," Orfe said. "That makes it hard for people to figure out what it is about me. My friends get used to it. Are we still friends?"

"I'd like that."

"Me too." Orfe drank at her glass of tea. "I missed you."

"No, you didn't," I told her.

"Did too."

"But you didn't—but I didn't miss you—"

"That's who I am," Orfe said, "and who you are."

"I figured you would have forgotten all about me. We were kids."

"How could I forget? We were kids," she said. "I guess a business degree just doesn't sound like you, Enny. Unless you've changed."

"Of course I've changed," I told her. "You helped."

"Just at the beginning."

"Once changes start, you know you can't keep them from moving along." I smiled again. "It feels, like, every year older I get the more I own myself. I like being older."

"Why, because kids are so helpless?"

"You were never helpless. Were you?"

She shrugged, lowered her head, raised her face to me. It had never crossed her mind to be helpless.

I wanted her to understand. "I don't see why commercial success can't be . . . virtuous or . . . honorable. Do you? There are companies that are successful and also good employers, good corporate citizens too. You don't have to be avaricious just because you're making money, do you?"

"I wouldn't know," she said.

"Like Ben and Jerry's," I said. "Like the Body Shop, like—" I stopped myself. "Isn't that what you wanted me to be like?"

"Depends," Orfe said.

"Depends on what?" I was getting irritated. "Anyway, I don't care," I said. "It's what I want for myself."

"Well, then," Orfe said. She stopped the waitress and asked for a cup of coffee. I asked for the same. "Are you sure it's okay if I stay with you? I don't have any bad habits, in case you're wondering—"

It hadn't crossed my mind.

"The school won't object?"

The school wouldn't care, I assured her.

"Then I'd be grateful. It would be a help, and fun too."

"Good." I waited, feeling talked out. It was Orfe's turn. "Aren't you going to tell me?"

"Tell you what?"

"How do I know? All I know is, you said you'd tell me while we ate."

"Oh." She seemed abstracted, watching her fingers pick up potato chips.

"And we've finished eating," I said.

"It's not much, nothing much, and I was thinking about something else—running into you again because—I heard on the radio, somewhere, a while ago . . . They found a warehouse, in some city in Vietnam, and stacked up in it, in the warehouse, like . . . like boxes of stereos in a warehouse, or bags of flour, there were bodies. Skeletons. With tags tied to their big toes, with dog tag numbers on their toes. And I was thinking, each one of them was having a life, his own life. And I was thinking, most of them were our age, probably."

"Probably most of them were black too," I told her, my voice thick.

"Oh, shit," Orfe said. "I never thought of that, but you're right."

"Or Indian," I said, making myself keep after the truth.

I watched the top of Orfe's head after that, making myself face the picture she had put before my mind's eye. After a pretty long time, she asked, "How'd you like it?"

"Like what?"

"My performance."

"I only heard the very end." I tried to remember my exact impressions. "Your voice is wonderful, but you must already know that. I never heard that song before."

"Because it's original."

"I only heard the very end," I apologized. "So you still want to be a musician? Can you earn enough to live on, on the streets? I don't mean that the way it sounds."

"I can. I lived a couple of years all over Europe that way. But—I just joined up with a band. The lead singer asked me, and I said okay, so—we've played a couple of gigs, we've got one coming up, I'm thinking about asking you if you want to see it. But—"

After a while, "But what?" I asked.

"Oh . . . It's metal, and I'm not sure how you feel about metal. We're a metal band, Jack and the Jackets—don't say it, Enny, okay?"

I didn't.

"And we're not very good. We're okay good but not nearly good enough. Not nearly as good as I am by myself." She wasn't apologizing, she was explaining. "And your opinion—what you think matters to me."

Orfe leaned forward to tell me about it.

"The drummer could be good, if only he'd work. I mean *work,* you know what I mean? Not just . . . Just because you have more talent than most people doesn't mean you don't have to work at it. The rest of them don't matter, they don't bother me, but Smiley could be really good if he'd just stop waiting around for whatever it is he expects will be given to him. Just given. Like some Christmas present from Santa, just given stark free. You know? Or if he'd stop looking for the high that will—be the angel he can ride where no drummer has ever gone before. Making him famous and rich. Or something. It makes me mad," Orfe said.

"You haven't changed much."

"Neither have you, really. Have you?"

I laughed. "Not if you don't think so."

"I don't. Other than growing up, of course," Orfe said. "Other than growing. I do want you to come hear us. Hear me, I mean. Would you? You want to? Do you mind pretty hard-core music?"

I decided not to lie. "That doesn't matter."

"I hope," Orfe said.

▲▲▲▲▲

Mushroom clouds in a row lined the walls of the room, shining in the dim light, fluorescent green mushroom clouds, fluorescent orange, fluorescent yellow. Small tables crowded back against the wall, across the room from the narrow wooden platform that made itself a stage by being elevated on wooden crates. Black amplifiers gleamed at the sides of the stage against a brick wall; silver microphones stood guard over the arrangement of drums and cymbals and pedals; wiring lay coiled black and shiny. I was taken to the girlfriends' table by the door. The room was so crowded and noisy that even if I had felt any inclination to talk, it wouldn't have been possible. Four spotlights burned overhead.

When a group of people, Orfe among them, worked their way through the crowd and mounted the stage, they were greeted with hoots and whistles. They wore black leather boots and black leather jackets; they wore belts, bracelets, and anklets of silvery studs fixed into black leather. The lead singer wore black leather trousers and a strip of white, like a skunk's stripe, in his long, dark hair. He stood in a spotlight, stage center. He raised his arm straight overhead, pointing, then lowered his stiff arm to point at the drummer, who flourished his sticks and played a roll, concluding with a thwack on the cymbals. The band played.

It felt as if the room were a moving vehicle and had just crashed up against a wall of sound. It felt as if a wall of sound had fallen into the room. Sound pulsed up, trapped in the small space, the drum pounding along beside the electric bass. The lead's voice slipped between drum and bass, riding the guitars—the voices of the audience rose in competition.

I couldn't listen because I couldn't hear. The room was too small, the amplifiers too powerful, the audience too inattentive. I wished myself elsewhere.

But I was there to see Orfe. She had her hair jammed into a black knit hat, and she was placed to one side of the platform. She attended only to the guitar under her hands, the left hand motionless on the neck, the fingers of the right moving on the strings in an unvarying pattern. The lead singer—Jack, I assumed—dominated the stage because he moved on it, hips fluid, long hair thrown from one side to the other, back and forth, his eyes most often closed as he screamed out the anger of his song.

The standing crowd swayed and chanted, "Not me, you won't get me." Some groups danced, sometimes slamming into one another. "Black man, red man, Chinaman's chance." Jack's face twisted into grimaces, his eyes squeezed shut, and his free hand reached desperately for the zipper of his jacket, which in the extreme of his emotion he pulled down and up, down and up. Number followed number. Every song seemed unwilling to end.

Finally, Jack pointed to Orfe. She took off the hat and shook her head. Her hair shone coppery red. She lay down the guitar and brought only the microphone forward with her. The audience quieted, anticipating.

"It's too soon," one voice from the crowd said. "I couldn't 've waited anymore," another spoke. "Maybe she won't—," a third asked. I looked but couldn't distinguish who was speaking. It was hot by then and close, sweaty, the air dense with the acrid gray smell of tobacco and the muskier, greener odor of pot. The band's instruments were muted, even the drum; this number seemed to be a duet, a lamentation for two voices, a dialogue between the two voices, almost merely a list of words Jack chanted, to which Orfe responded in chorus. It sounded like Jack was chanting newspaper headlines. "It makes me sick," Orfe sang in response, never looking away from his face, "It makes me sick." He leaned toward her, microphone touching his lips, as if he loved his words.

More and more Orfe accompanied her line of choric song with an odd hunching gesture of her shoulders.

Then she stumbled, almost doubled over. When she started to vomit I rose in my chair—

"What're you doing?" one of the girlfriends asked.

"She's sick, I—"

Her hand tethered me to the table and forced me back into my seat. "Cool it. You want to ruin the show? Kee-rist," she said, disgusted. I was out of place, stupid. The girlfriend's hand was locked around my wrist. I didn't know if I ought to be trying to twist free. I didn't know why she was telling me to shut up. I didn't know anything.

Meanwhile, on the platform, the song went on. Jack chanted headlines. Sometimes Orfe sang the chorus through, sometimes she just threw up, sometimes she got two or three words out before—

The audience crowded close, as if asking to be spattered. "It makes me *sick,*" they sang along.

And I remembered that Orfe used to be able to throw up at will, and I sat back—

It was not pleasant to watch. It didn't even go on that long, Orfe didn't even projectile vomit that many times—

But then there's only so much food you can cram into your stomach—isn't there?—so you can vomit it out.

—but even so, however cynical my thoughts, I had to notice that by the end Orfe looked as if she were actually sick, pasty-faced, her hair a tangled mess, spattered—her eyes not focusing on anything in the room—her mouth slack, as she wiped her hand across it to try to go on singing as if . . . as if the song were true.

The audience loved it. "Whoo yeah yeah, you *know*

it, tell it like it is, baby, me too, me too, Ooowhee." The room rang with applause.

"That's it." The girlfriend's voice came close to my ear. "Are you okay?"

I wasn't, but I wasn't about to tell her. I didn't know what I could do about it anyway; I couldn't do anything.

The audience pushed close, trapping the performers on the stage. I heard voices: "I never felt . . ." "not ever before . . ." "felt . . ." "never felt before—"

"Sometimes, the first time," the girlfriend said, quietly, almost friendly now, "people—it makes them a little sick, you know? Nobody actually has, but lots of people think—*are* you okay?"

I nodded my head, although I felt sick, and I wished I could be sick to get rid of that feeling, because how I felt and why I felt that way—well—vomiting seemed to me to be the only response that had any integrity.

I remembered again that Orfe could make herself throw up.

I asked her that night, back in my dormitory room. Orfe had showered and wrapped herself up in my bathrobe, still pale but sitting cross-legged on my bed, holding an acoustic guitar in her lap, the music flowing out of it, floating. "Are you faking it, Orfe?" I asked.

Orfe didn't answer. Her hands drew music from the guitar and after a while she asked me, "You want to hear one of my songs?"

By then I was unwilling to interrupt the sound of the guitar even by my own voice speaking only one syllable.

"I hate it," Orfe mumbled, and I knew what she meant by *it*.

I nodded. I didn't care what she said. Her words had no meaning, no importance—as long as the music went on; it didn't matter what I thought or feared or doubted, as long as the music went on; as long as the music went on, everything would be all right; nothing signified, everything could be lost, but as long as the music went on . . .

"Listen."

She played all that night, song after song, all from memory. I listened, tireless. By morning, when the fresh young air came in through the grimy window, when Orfe stopped playing, singing, my room was filled with people, as was the hallway beyond. Then she answered my question: "I don't know."

▲▲▲▲▲

The difference is that nobody ever wanted to say to Orfe, "You were terrific." Even when she was in the spotlight, "What a song," they would say and never "What a singer." Most often they would say nothing because speech hinders hearing. All words can do is tell the feelings. My feeling was: I didn't want the music to end, not once, not ever. I felt embraced, empowered. Secure in my own strength. Enchanted. Humbled, made into nothing. Exalted. I felt released from the prison of myself.

▲▲▲▲▲

Once I had found her again, I never missed hearing Orfe perform, even with Jack and the Jackets, whom I disliked more each time I heard them, and saw them, especially the duet. They called it "Current Events," but the audience called out for it under the name of "It Makes Me Sick." There's no way around it. The duet was the purpose of every performance: Jack pursued her with words and eventually, inevitably, Orfe threw up. The audience expected that finale, anticipated it, stopped dancing and crowded up around the platform, breathing with the driving drums and words until it happened—after which the audience sighed, satisfied. Then they returned to tables, finished drinks, gathered up belongings, murmuring or silent, and left.

Afterward Orfe stood, not even accepting applause, while the band and Jack bowed, grinned, applauded themselves. She stood still, her skin white, her copper hair glowing like a crown. We would go back to my dormitory room, Orfe and I, and they would be waiting—in the reception room, along the halls, in my room unless I had remembered to lock the door, sprawled on my bed in a tangle of legs, sprawled on the floor, at the chair at my desk, and on the windowsill. I had classes to go to and courses to pass, so Orfe would lead everyone out into the reception room. I thought at first that I wouldn't be able to sleep; I thought the music would call me out of bed, but I was wrong. It seemed as if the music took me by the hand, and I was asleep almost the minute my head went down on the pillow. I slept long and deep, and I rose refreshed from those nights. In the mornings I sat up in bed to see Orfe asleep on the floor, a giant caterpillar in the cocoon of her sleeping bag, her bright hair snarled into elflocks by the exertions of her day and her night and her sleep.

Jack and the Jackets played every other week, then every week, then two nights a week. Orfe could no longer manage the walk home, or even the steps up into a bus, so we took taxis. She seemed, coming offstage, pale and strengthless. People still waited for her return to the dormitory, in still increasing numbers, and she played her own songs for whatever remained of the night and whatever remained of her strength.

I tried to talk sense to her, but she didn't hear me. I was carrying her guitar by then and her black leather airman's jacket. One night she was so exhausted she stumbled into the glass door. The crowd didn't say anything or move in any direction; they stood and waited for the music to begin.

I lost my temper. I'd had it with everyone, Jack the egomaniac and Orfe the martyr and the waiting crowd before me and the panting crowd we'd left behind. "She's not going to play tonight," I announced. "Everybody go away. Not tomorrow either. I'll let you know when. I'll post a notice. I'll post a notice on the bulletin board in Main." They didn't question my words or my right to pronounce. They drifted away. Nobody complained. Nobody minded, it seemed, as long as there was a future performance promised.

That night I put Orfe into my bed and took the sleeping bag for myself. She didn't notice where she was. She slept with her arms flung out, exhausted. I sat up for a while, a textbook in front of me as if I were studying. I wasn't studying. I was just sitting, arms wrapped around my knees, waiting to be tired enough to sleep.

I did sleep, eventually, and woke and went to classes, and when I returned Orfe was sitting on my bed. "Don't do that again," she said.

"Do what?"

"Give me your bed. If you do that, I'll have to move out. Do you want to be my manager? Remember, we talked about it?"

"What?" I emptied my armload of books onto the made bed. "You mean back then? That was just kids talking. I'm a full-time student, I'm going for a degree. *Orfe,*" I repeated, "that was years and years ago, and besides, I don't know anything about it."

She was at my desk. "You're smart enough, you could do it and still go for your degree."

She was right about that. I hadn't known that, but once Orfe pointed it out to me I knew she was right.

"But I don't know anything, I wouldn't know how to do anything. Or work with Jack," I admitted. "I don't like—" I couldn't begin to make a list of all the things I didn't like about Jack and his band. "I don't like—"

"The first time, Jack didn't know. That's the truth," Orfe said. "At first he had no idea what would happen, but ever since then—I do try," she said. "But he pushes the words into my stomach, they ride in on the music? He says the audience needs it."

"Do you believe that?"

"I don't know. Sometimes I think I just act out what they feel, what they're feeling, sometimes. The ones who come more than once—it can't be shock value anymore. I can feel them waiting, wanting, hoping. . . . You don't know."

"You're right, I don't."

"Asking me to do it, for them, so they won't have to do it for themselves? Because they can't? I don't have any choice."

"You could quit."

"I can't. That's why you should be my manager."

She came back to the subject more than once. And "I can't quit," she said, more than once.

"What do you mean?" I finally asked. "You're not afraid of anyone. Are you? You never were. Or anything."

"It's not about being afraid," Orfe said. Her head was bent down, her face hidden.

I'd only been thinking about why I couldn't be anyone's manager. Now I asked her, "I don't understand."

Her hair moved as she nodded her head; she agreed with me. "Whenever I tell Jack I'm quitting, he says he's sorry, he says he wants me to stay, he says he'll do a couple of my songs and we won't do 'Current Events.' "

"I'll just bet he does," I said. "And how many times has he made that promise?"

"And he always means it," Orfe's voice said. "He does, I know he does. Then when he's out there, when we're actually doing the show, he doesn't do what he said. Up until he doesn't do it, he means to. But the audience wants . . . Jack can't help it. I feel sorry for him."

"What about you?" I was beginning to wonder if having me for manager might not be preferable to having no manager. "Don't you feel sorry for yourself?"

Orfe lifted her face and her eyes spoke to me. She didn't need to say it, but she did, "Ashamed."

"Okay, I'll try it. I'll try managing you," I decided, the quickest decision of my life. "I'll talk to Jack. What kind of a contract did you sign?"

"No contract."

"Orfe, without a contract, you can leave whenever you want."

"Jack says all I've got going for me is a pair of tits and an okay voice."

I stared at her. "Do you believe that?"

"Mostly not."

"He's lying. The guy's an asshole."

Orfe grinned at me. "I know that, and you know that, but what if he isn't?"

"Your voice is better than okay," I pointed out. "Much better than okay." But Jack was a professional, and he'd been in the business for years. "Isn't it?"

"Yes," Orfe said. As I talked myself out of confidence, she gained it.

"And your tits—"

She started to laugh. "Aren't much at all. I'm not faking it," she told me. "I always mean it, every time. I can't help it—When he sings those words at me, I can't help swallowing them, and feeling them, and it makes me sick. I promise. I wouldn't do it if I were faking it. I'd get a job flipping hamburgers and never write another song, never sing again, if I had to fake anything. You've known me longer than anyone, you should know that."

"I do."

Orfe watched my face. "You do believe me?"

"I do."

"Because if you don't, I don't think anybody should."

"I'll be your manager. I'll talk to Jack. If I can, I'll do everything I can."

The next day I wore a suit to classes, my pin-striped job interview suit, and met Jack for coffee on the way back. I put my books and notebooks authoritatively down on the table beside me and announced bluntly that Orfe was quitting the band. Then I sat tense, looking—I hoped—calm.

Jack offered no resistance.

"I knew it." He stirred his coffee. "I knew she'd do this to me. It's that guy, isn't it?"

What guy? But I didn't ask. You did it to yourself, I didn't say. All I did was take out of my notebook the release form I'd spent lunch hour in the school library writing and typing up in triplicate. I passed all three copies across to Jack and offered him my ballpoint pen. "Sign here and here and here."

"You don't know about Yuri? She hasn't told you?"

"You ought to read this before you sign it," I advised.

"As a friend of hers, I oughtta tell you, warn you. He's bad cess," Jack said. "I tried to tell her, but you can't tell Orfe anything. Where do I sign? I can't sign fast enough. But she doesn't need this, we never had any contract written down, whatever she's told you."

"Then it doesn't matter that you sign," I said. Patiently. The release was an extra safeguard for Orfe, in case Jack ever decided it would be worth his while to come along with a lawyer and sue.

He scrawled his name, once, twice, three times, and

shoved the papers back toward me. I signed one and gave it back to him. He studied it. "What am I going to do?" he asked. "What about me?"

I didn't meet his eyes. I gathered together the papers and kept my face expressionless, as if I were invulnerable to pity. When Jack spoke again, I was glad to hear bitterness. "You're going to be her manager, is that it? That's a joke. I'll get a lot of laughs out of that, the two of you, no idea at all what the game is really like. You've got no idea how tough it is."

I put the papers in the notebook, closed the notebook over them, and left.

▲▲▲▲▲

So I became Orfe's manager. If I had known then what I know now, I never would have. But what I know now I learned then.

Just for example: The first thing was to get her listened to. You can't sit around, waiting to be discovered, you have to put yourself forward; or you have to have a manager to put you forward—that is, when your manager isn't busy keeping up with the work of her education so she'll be able to do little things in her life like keep food on the table and pay the rent. As manager, my first task was to get Orfe listened to.

I don't think there's any ignorance I missed. I bought a tape, borrowed a tape deck, had Orfe sing into it. . . . Even *I* could hear that it wouldn't do. Then I discovered that everybody, or everybody's brother, has a friend who knows something, knows someone. . . . And it took me a while to learn that everybody can't be relied on, not for more than genuinely wishing you well, sometimes. I ran in circles for a while, before I learned how to find a recording studio and rent time, what kind of equipment I needed so we could make a good-quality tape and who I could borrow it from, what kind of equipment I needed to play the finished tape for whomever I was asking to listen to Orfe.

Orfe never lost patience, never lost hope, never lost faith in me. She earned regular money and slept in my room occasionally. I finally asked her about Yuri and she told me. "He's my guy, he's my lover, he's . . ."

"Bad cess, Jack said," I finished her sentence, "which I take it means an addict. What is he, recovering?" hoping she would deny it.

"—beautiful, he likes my songs, he wants to meet you."

"Sure," I said. "Whenever." I waited for Orfe to name the time and place. She didn't say anything. "But where do you think I should take this tape to play it?" Orfe had no idea.

Everybody else had suggestions and ideas, people their sisters knew. . . . In the end, I went to places where I thought Orfe might have a chance.

Talk about learning experiences. Learning how to dress, what to say, just so somebody would agree to listen to a song, just one song. Most of the somebodies were men, but that was about all they had in common. I learned—as fast as I could—how to recognize the person who could actually make the decision, whether or not to haul the tape forthrightly out of my purse or to try to lead the conversation around to the point where he might ask me if I had one; I learned who resented and who preferred jeans on his suppliants, who thought that if you didn't say *fuck* and *fucking*, you weren't worth listening to, and who thought that if you did, that was something you were willing to do to get your tape listened to; I learned how to recognize an implacable *no!* and when I could press a little harder, just in case.

All to no avail.

On the best days I would finally get to play the tape and the face would listen politely, and then turn from side to side: No, sorry.

I finally admitted that however clear and good they were, the tapes didn't convince anybody that he wanted to hire Orfe, so the tapes weren't good enough. "Come see her perform in front of an audience," I'd say. "You have to see her in live performance."

"Where's she playing?"

I'd name the street corner, but that was a kiss of death, playing on the streets. "Listen, sweetie, I'd like to help you, you look like a nice girl, but, you know, singers are a dime a dozen, I could get singers—and good singers, like your friend on the tape—just by snapping my fingers twice. Just like this. She needs a band, is what. It's easier to book a band. People want to hear a whole performance, not just a singer. You know what I mean? Thanks for stopping in, for asking me. Tell your friend she needs a band."

Those were the polite ones. The not-so-polite ones just said, "Give me a break, will you?"

▲▲▲▲▲

"You need a band," I told Orfe.

"You think?"

"No, not personally."

"You sound tired, Enny. Your grades are okay, aren't they?"

"Never better." That was the truth. I'd never done better work with less effort. "I can't figure out why, except—you're a good influence on me. Either that or I'm the kind of person who does best when she's overworked."

"You're not overworked," Orfe quickly pointed out. A stickler.

"But I have no idea how to find a band."

"Look for it, that's the first step."

"A whole band?"

"Probably not, probably we'd have better luck looking for solos," Orfe said. "If you know where to look."

"Do you know where to look?"

"I could ask, when I play, maybe someone listening—but it'll have to be *my* songs."

Orfe's face was hidden, lowered, and then she raised her head. Eager, she was so glad for what was coming up next in her life she could give it away. With anyone else I might have envied that much gladness, but for Orfe, being glad wasn't something that made other people jealous. It was like her songs: When Orfe sang about the homeless, for example, I always went out and did something—took food into a shelter or found some clothes

I'd never use again or just smiled and said hello to someone clawing her way through a garbage can as if I could tell the difference between her and the garbage her hands were in. It wasn't just me, either, responding that way. You could see it. Orfe's songs made a difference, an actual, acted-out difference. Orfe's eager gladness got to me. "A band will come along," she said.

"Be real," I advised her, also myself.

"I'll be looking too."

"What about Yuri, could he play?"

She shook her head. "I don't want to ask him. I don't even want him to know I'm looking. He's got his hands full staying clean right now. He'd want to help out, and it would be his old friends he'd think of, and his old friends live the old way in the old place. . . . Not Yuri."

My boyfriend of the time knew something about music. In fact, it was his interest in Orfe's music that led him to me, so he was happy to join the search for backup instruments and singers. We went to clubs and bars, parks, and the occasional college organization party, keeping our ears open for someone who might do for Orfe, a musician looking for a group to play with and songs, a group looking for a singer and songs.

And we were the ones who found the bass player, Grace Phildon. In actual fact, it was Zach—that was his name, Zachary, a great name, Zachary Cairn, I wonder sometimes what happened to him. We stayed friends right through graduation, long after we'd decided we weren't meant to be lovers and wouldn't ever be. Then after graduation Zach went to Europe, and I lost touch with him.

It was Zach who found Grace Phildon, but not in any of the likely places where we had gone looking for musicians. He found her on the notice board of the local deli-grocery-news-and-magazine store, while I was picking up salad for a late supper and some bread to go with it. Zach saw the card and called me over. "Something about this gets me," he said.

Something about it got me too. Maybe the bold black strokes out of which name, instrument, and phone number were formed. Maybe the lack of any further information on the card. We told Orfe, and she called to set up a meeting. "An audition," I corrected, taking the phone away from Orfe and introducing myself, "the manager."

"Makes never no mind to me what you call it," the voice responded. "I'll be there." She read back the address. "I'll be on time." She repeated the time.

"So will we," I promised.

▲▲▲▲▲

Grace Phildon was prompt—a knock at the door, which Orfe went to open, as if I were the one running the audition. As if I were the one who would know and decide. "Orfe," I protested, following, and Grace Phildon pushed open the door. She wore jeans and a red sweatshirt; she had a bass guitar in its case in one hand and a child at the other. She was young to have a child in hand, even a child like this one just starting to walk; she was no older than we were. The child was diapers, dark curly hair, and satiny brown skin. "I apologize for having the baby with me. My mother wasn't free and my sisters have jobs. If that gripes you, I can leave right now. Usually I don't have my baby with me. Usually I make arrangements."

"Doesn't bother me," Orfe said. I shook my head, it didn't bother me. For all I knew, that might be the standard way of doing an audition.

Grace Phildon lifted the child into a corner of a deep chair. "You got to sit quiet while Mommy makes a little music. Can you be good, honey?"

The little head nodded. A thumb went into the mouth. Grace Phildon straightened up, a sturdy figure, solid legs, broad torso, strong arms. "I can sing, I can play, I can dance, sort of. What do you want?"

Orfe went to the upright piano and played a classic Beatles song, "Blackbird." Grace Phildon's voice was soft, and warm, and sat lightly on the air. When Orfe joined in, Grace Phildon switched to singing harmony, the two voices blending like a warm breeze and sunny air.

She sounded good to me, the two of them sounded good. They took out their instruments and played "American Pie," sounding good, guitar and bass, unamplified, singing. "Do you read music?" Orfe asked.

"Some. I've been studying—some."

They played one of Orfe's songs, playing it through time after time until it came smooth. I sat and listened, as content as the baby.

"Okay," Orfe said at last. "Here's what we're talking about. I'm looking to form a band to back me up, doing mostly my own songs, like that one." Grace Phildon waited for the list to be complete. "Equal split on any money, including the manager gets an equal share. Drugs are out, absolutely, and no funny stuff about it," Orfe said. "My guy is a recovering addict."

"No problem," Grace said. "I see no problem with any of it."

"I don't have any work, not yet. No jobs to offer you."

"I figured. Or else why would you have seen my notice? I'm happy to bank on you, and so's Cass, aren't you, honey?" The baby had slid down, while they sang, and trundled over, while they sang and played, to plunk itself down on the floor and listen from up close. "I had to leave school with Cass," Grace said, "and I figure, my talent is my only hope for me. You—you're some kind of music, and if you'd like me, I sure would like you."

Orfe said, "I wish we had some jobs to offer."

"We're fine, Cass and me, we've got family, I work at one of the hamburger joints—flexible hours, no problem. For the baby's life too, I mean. I mean, hope."

▲▲▲▲▲

The second band member Orfe brought in from the street. There was no audition. There was no consultation with Grace Phildon or with me. That day Orfe arrived in the dormitory reception room where Grace was waiting for a rehearsal session, and I was keeping Grace company. A few minutes after Orfe arrived another person showed up, toting a big black box of an amplifier. She set it down and left without a word, to come back a couple of minutes later carrying a guitar. In those minutes Orfe had said, "Willie. I asked her to be in the band," and I had said, "I thought I was your manager, I thought a manager was consulted, I thought I had a voice in decisions." And Orfe said, "About music? About my music?" as if that were a thought so bizarre she'd never even thought to think of it before. And I said, "I'm sorry," immediately afraid that now Orfe had thought of it she'd dump me, and Orfe said, "Don't be stupid, do you think it would be better that way?" and Grace Phildon spoke for the first time. "Dunno about better, but it's the usual way. Usually there's a couple of good reasons—along with the usual bad ones—for the usual way of doing things." "You'd have liked it if I had talked it over with you first?" Orfe asked. Grace nodded. Orfe looked at me. I nodded. Then Orfe nodded, agreeing. "Her last name's Grace," Orfe said. "Willie Grace. She's really good."

Willie Grace interrupted us, all sharp angles of elbows and chin and hips, jet black eyes sharp as coals, the corners of her mind and tongue as sharp as bones. "You-all unhappy with me? I can be outta here in about two minutes flat. Fuck it, that's what I say."

Hostility you could touch was in the air, so sharp you could cut your fingers on it if you put your fingers out. I was silent. Grace Phildon was silent.

"Anyway, let's try a song," Orfe said.

"I mean it," Willie Grace said. She hadn't even plugged her guitar into the amplifier. "I don't need any bad-mouthing from any wussy females."

I didn't like her. "I thought *wussy* was a gender-specific put-down," I said.

"Let's do a song and just hear how we sound," Orfe asked again.

We ignored her. Willie Grace put her hand on her hip and jutted her elbow out, her hip jutted out. "Yeah? Oh, yeah? You mean, like, I can't call you a prick even when you're acting like one?"

Orfe laughed. I didn't blame her.

"I wouldn't have thought you'd have this kind of friend, Orfe," Willie Grace said.

"Only one," Orfe said. "I never met anyone else like Enny."

I could stand up for myself. "What do you mean by that?" I demanded of Willie Grace.

"College," Willie Grace said. "But lemme tell you, college kid, maybe I did get this little black ass out of school the day I turned sixteen, but I passed the GED the next day. Going to college doesn't mean anything."

"Tell me about it," I said.

She looked at me.

"Neither does not going to college," I said.

She looked at me.

"Can we play now?" Orfe asked.

Willie Grace shrugged. "What've I got to lose," she said, eyeing Orfe, eyeing Grace Phildon, ignoring me. "I can read music," she said, plugged in and ready, her hand out and waiting.

They played a song, once, then again, then a third perfect time, then again, and again, and again, each time more perfect than the perfect time before. When they stopped, Willie Grace wheeled around on the other two—all of them had forgotten me; I sat on the floor drowning five fathoms deep in song—"You try to get rid of me and I'll . . . I'll bust up your appearances. I can do it. I'm not embarrassed to be a spectacle."

"Why would I want to get rid of you? I don't, Grace, do you?" Grace Phildon didn't. And I didn't. I didn't even remember how it felt to not want Willie Grace in the band.

"She's got the right name," Orfe pointed out.

"It must be fate," I agreed.

"What name? Willie?" Willie Grace asked.

"Grace," I told her.

"What?" Grace Phildon asked.

"And I hope the three of you have a lot of free time the next four days," I announced, this seeming an appropriate time to take the ace out of my pocket and lay it down in front of them all, "because you've been hired to play a dance."

"Hired, as in: Money will change hands?" Willie Grace asked.

I told them how much. How little, actually.

"Divided three ways?" Willie Grace asked.

"Four," I said.

"You get a quarter?"

"We all get equal."

"Yeah? What do you do that's so important?"

"Whatever needs doing."

We stared at each other. Her eyes glittered. I don't know what she saw other than that I wasn't about to bend over and let her kick me, the way she wanted to. I held her eyes long enough and then broke the connection. I couldn't stay there all day. I had work to do, readings to complete, case studies to analyze so that I could argue my conclusions and solutions before a class. I turned to leave.

"A dance?" Orfe protested. "How come a dance, Enny?"

"It's a job," I said.

"But—I thought we were—a concert."

"I've been trying."

She didn't doubt me. "Or performance or—"

"I can't do that for you. Orfe, you don't have to keep me on, there are lots of people who might be able—" She was shaking her head. We were talking sort of quietly, just the two of us. "If I could just get someone to come and listen, I think that would do it—or another tape. I want to do another tape, if that's okay, now that you've got a band."

"I'm thinking of three instruments, a three-piece band. With the Graces, we've already got two; I was thinking another woman."

"Somebody named Grace, right?"

"That would be too much of a coincidence. But—what if someone did, it would seriously start to feel—wouldn't it?"

"Seriously? It would seriously make me feel crazy. But how do all-women bands do? Has there ever—?"

Orfe had no idea, and the odds made no difference to her; she wanted to get back to the rehearsal. Playing. Singing. The music. "I knew you'd like Willie," Orfe said, then shut the door behind me.

They played the dance, and out of that came another job offer. Another dance, but as it turned out, Orfe didn't mind playing dances. As it turned out, she liked seeing people dance to her music. "Sorry about giving you lip," she said to me. "I honestly didn't know, I honestly thought—"

"Thought what?"

"Thought—I didn't know this until right now, I give you my word, if I had known—I thought, when I pictured it, I had to be at the spotlight, at the microphone, at the center. The Lead Singer, you know? I must have caught it from Jack."

"Him and the rest of the world."

"Because it's really about music."

"Because it's easier to think that you know what's going on," I realized, "when you put one person in the spotlight and make them the star. If you do that, you feel like someone knows what's going on, someone is in control—instead of the way it is—"

"It's really about whatever makes the music. Including the part of music you can't ever figure out," Orfe explained to me.

"—with some people doing some things well, understanding some things, but nobody knowing everything. If you try to make it into one person who does and understands everything best, then you're just asking to be let down, aren't you? And you're forcing them to fail, because nobody can—" I didn't know what kind of a friend I was to Orfe, expecting as much as I did. "I know what you mean," I said to her.

"There never will be only one center stage," Orfe said. "I know what you mean."

I taped a couple of their rehearsals, and my boyfriend of the time, still Zach, edited the tapes into ten minutes of uninterrupted music. I made myself do the rounds again—between classes and schoolwork and listening in on rehearsals. On those rounds I saw some of the same people and some I hadn't seen before. Some of my previous contacts I didn't want ever to be in the same room with again, and some of them had folded up their tents and gotten into something else, somewhere else. The only real difference was that now some of the people knew who Orfe was, either because they remembered me or because they had heard of us.

Nobody listened to the tape all the way through, however, and nobody asked where he or she could see the band live. "You need a regular place to play," they advised me. "Regular appearances. See, if a band is good enough to draw a regular crowd, then it's worth my going to hear. See what I mean?"

"But you told me—"

I tried again: "If they do, and I let you know where and when, will you come hear them?"

"Hey, sugar, bet your boobies," or some such phrase, and some of them meant it. "See, a tape can get itself doctored. How do I know from a tape what the band really sounds like? These days you can't believe what you hear or see."

I stood mute-faced, communicating nothing.

"So get yourself a club, get that band of yours a club. That's my advice. For free, for once."

▲▲▲▲▲

The second dance brought in two job offers and suddenly we were in business. Once it had happened, it seemed as if it were inevitable, as if there were no way it couldn't have happened. We found a studio we could rent by the week, a small, almost windowless room, with lots of electric plugs and true acoustics. Practically the first day the band was rehearsing there—I was present to adjust amplifiers, to pick up sheets of music that fell at inconvenient times, to bring in food and drink, to listen—the door opened on us in the middle of a song.

The music dribbled away to a questioning silence.

It was a guy, a little round guy with reddish cheeks and yellowish hair and a green-striped shirt on with his jeans, a little apple of a guy with eyes that looked around glad. He had a guitar case and he looked at Orfe and the two Graces as if he expected them to be pleased to see him. "I heard you play," he said, to all of them but mostly Orfe. "I want to play with you."

There was a laying down of instruments (them) and a rising to feet (me). He unsnapped his case and took out his guitar, an electrified twelve-string.

"Sonny," Willie Grace said. "We're not jamming here. We're working. Rehearsing. Beat it, okay?"

"Name's not Sonny," he answered with no anger in his voice. "It's Ray."

"How did you find us?" Grace Phildon wondered.

"I asked around. I tracked you down. It's not such a big world."

"Your last name isn't Grace, by any chance . . . is it?" Orfe asked.

"Why?" he asked.

She didn't tell him. "We're not looking for—"

He stood eye level with Orfe, round and unperturbed as an apple. "Tell me what you're looking for and I could be it. I'm pretty resilient."

"You're too deaf to hear the word *no*?" Willie Grace asked. "The word is *no*, Ray. Ray what, what's your name?"

"Grace," Ray said.

"Liar," Willie Grace said. "Out."

"First, I play. You'd do the same."

It wasn't a question. Willie Grace shrugged and faded from the argument.

"I'm sorry," Orfe said to him.

He plugged his guitar in and put on metal finger picks.

"I mean it," Orfe said.

"We could let him just play, don't you think?" I asked, wanting, for some reason I couldn't define, things to go well for him. "Is there any reason he can't audition?"

He didn't wait for more encouragement. He started playing a piece I remembered from piano lessons, "In a Country Garden," about the first piece anyone learns. He played the melody line first, then added a harmony line, then switched to a folk-style arpeggio backup, a country-and-western four-beat, and a blues rendering that meandered over a walking bass, then a twanging rock, the strings vibrating over a pulsing bass line that had my hips and shoulders moving in rhythm. You couldn't help but smile. All four of us were smiling, glad-hearted at listening to him make his joke. At the end he grinned around at us, hands still, guitar silent. "Also, I do 'Greensleeves.' "

"That was fun," Orfe said. "But now, if you'll excuse us—?"

He unplugged and turned away, accepting her decision.

"But, Orfe, why not?" I asked. "Why not at least play a song all together, to hear how it goes? Why not just try? Because he's not female? Or black? I don't understand. His name's Grace," I pointed out.

"I don't exactly believe that," she said.

"It's not exactly true," he said at the same time. "It just—seemed to matter, so I figured, if I wanted a chance to try out."

Orfe nodded to him, eye to eye.

"Stop me if I'm wrong," he said, "but I think I'd sound good with you, I think my playing and my voice would mix well with the rest of you."

Orfe said, "That's for me to decide."

"I'm not saying I know better than you," Ray not-Grace said. "But I'm not going to let you say you know better than me either."

Orfe hesitated. "We'll try it—but with conditions," she said.

"Like what?" he asked.

"We do my songs," she said.

"Am I supposed to mind that?"

"No drugs. Do you do drugs?"

"Why should I?"

"Money is split equally between all band members and manager."

"Sounds fair."

"It's only on trial," Orfe said.

"Listen, I can change my name," he said. "It's easy, I just did it, added a middle name—no, I want one of those Southern two-gun names. Raygrace. Abracadabra—be Raygrace," he said, throwing his hands up, as if he were releasing twin doves. "And it's done," he said. Willie Grace had already plugged him back in, and they got down to work.

▲▲▲▲▲

A band has to have a name, so between practice sessions—learning music, learning one another—they worried the question of a name. It was a way of winding down. They sat around the studio, sweaty, instruments closed away safely into cases, and quarreled about a name. Orfe and the Graces, that was my first suggestion the first time the question was raised.

"Boy, does that not grab me," Raygrace said. "What about Good Graces?"

"Good Gracious?"

"Amazing Graces?" Raygrace offered.

"That leaves me out," Orfe objected.

"Amazing Graces and Orfe?"

Groans greeted that idea.

"Goodness Gracious. Goodness and Gracious? You can be goodness, see, and we'll be gracious."

"Grace, Gracious, Graceless, and Ungrateful?"

"I'm not ungrateful," Orfe protested.

Orfe and the Graces was the name they adopted, until they could come up with something better. Just until. "It's only true," Raygrace said. "That's not nearly good enough."

"It'll do for starters," Grace Phildon said.

"I'd settle for ending up there too," Willie Grace said.

"Orfe and the Graces is not exactly catchy," Raygrace said. "How about Gracious Me?"

"You're not some fucking solo act," Willie Grace said. "And don't say what you're thinking, college kid," she said to me.

"Hey, I go to college too," Raygrace said.

Orfe and the Graces played one or two gigs a week, regularly, during that time, enough work to take a monthly lease of the studio, which gave us the space at a lower rate. Orfe kept a bedroll there, for nights when she didn't want to leave what she was working on. The studio came with a tiny bathroom—toilet and sink and cracked mirror. You could bring food in with you. The whole building was locked at midnight and each studio had its own locked door, so even though there was no watchman, it was reasonably safe. If Orfe wanted a shower, she came to my dorm or spent some time with Yuri at the halfway house. They were looking for an apartment of their own by then. Orfe and the Graces were doing well enough so that Orfe and Yuri could afford a place of their own. In fact, Raygrace and Willie Grace already shared an apartment by then. "Not the bed, though. This isn't a relationship," Willie Grace told us.

"Not that I'd mind," Raygrace said.

"I'd mind," she told him. "It'd be one thing then another with you. I know your type, you'd start in on me about making commitments."

"You're already committed," Raygrace told her. "You just won't admit it."

"The way men," Willie Grace said, "work women over, jerk them around."

"Depends on how you look at it," Grace Phildon joined in. "I got Cass out of the deal, and he didn't get much of anything."

"Only just exactly what he was looking for," Willie Grace said.

"But, honey, the point is, he wasn't looking for much of anything. He could of had himself a whole lot, but he didn't even know."

"What whole lot?"

"Why, me."

Orfe never said much, just sat listening. Her fingers fiddled around on the guitar. Her face was pale, her movements slower, clumsier; I thought she was burning herself out somehow, maybe in bed with Yuri, maybe she had some part-time job she hadn't told the rest of us about.

I was wrong about Orfe, though. She was writing music, writing songs. She wasn't burning herself out or burning herself up—she was on fire.

There were two kinds of music she was writing, both of them for the group but only one for immediate performance. She called the performance songs her fossil-fuel numbers, because they were the band's economic underpinnings. The band played them at the dances they were hired for by various organizations—fraternities, sororities, local clubs—or at private parties. Some of those songs had words, and after a while some of the dance-goers had come back frequently enough to sing along, but it was mostly foot-lifting, hip-hinging, arm-pulling music, for dancing. As long as the music played, all you wanted to do was dance, and you danced better than you ever had. Not everyone, of course; there is always someone to complain. Boys who hoped to get laid, after the music stopped but before it left the bloodstream, complained that it went on too long; faculty advisors complained that it went on too loud; girls who hoped to fall in love behind the seductive veil of music complained that it took too much of everyone's attention.

The other music Orfe was working on . . . That, she finally allowed the band to try out. It was songs, songs for concert performance. Orfe gave the Graces the music and they all worked out the arrangements. One day, at one dance, when they played the first of these songs—

—the dancers stopped and turned to the stage, caught. The dancers crowded up as close to the stage as they could get. The dancers swayed to the music, swayed toward the stage. *Yuri's Dreams*, Orfe called the new songs.

After that, dances the group played were also concerts. And concerts were also dances. There was no either/or, no playing either a concert or a dance, there was only playing. Orfe and the Graces moved out of a world of either/or. Orfe and the Graces played music.

They played in a hall of some kind, as a rule, an open hall or a gymnasium, somewhere roomy enough for an elevated stage to be put up, with space for dancing. Job offers came in almost daily, until I was turning down work without a second thought—if the space wasn't right, the time wasn't right, the money wasn't right, or if any one of us for some reason took against the way the job was offered or the persons who offered it. The band was performing four or five times a week and could have performed seven nights and two afternoons, regularly. After one gymnasium gig a man in a gray silk suit approached me, his hand held out not for me to shake but to give me his business card.

I put down the amplifier I was carrying. "They told me—you're the manager?"

He had a shifty look. His eyes didn't rest on any object or person. His eyes were busy looking for the main chance. "I'm wondering if you've cut a record? Or made a tape? Because I'd be happy to hustle it for you. I think your friends have got a future, and you must think the same. So what do you say, sweets? Do we cut the deal or what?"

Because I knew as soon as I saw his eyes that I would say no to whatever he asked, it was as if I had already spoken the word out loud. I was distracted by thinking about what his offer meant. My hesitation gave him hope. Seeing him have hope made me feel bad about leading him on. I cut short his smile. "No. No, thanks."

"You're making a big mistake," he warned me.

I didn't want to talk to him. I was wondering how many of Orfe's songs she would think had gotten to final form, how many she would say were ready to be recorded. "Ummnnnmm," I said.

"So you'll think about it?" he asked, thinking he'd been successful after all.

I shook my head.

"Big mistake, sweets. Really big mistake. Don't say I didn't warn you. People in this business, they eat little girls like you for breakfast. For between-meal snacks. Good bands miss out on all their chances, if the manager doesn't know—I could tell you some stories that would make you weep."

I shook my head. I picked up the amplifier, and he didn't offer a hand. "Keep the card. You'll be calling, begging for help."

Later that night I asked Orfe about it. "There was this guy, some promoter, after the show. He asked me if you'd cut a record, if he could get in on the action. What about a record, Orfe, what do you think?"

Orfe took a minute before she lifted her face: She looked like I'd just handed her the Nobel Peace Prize, gladness pouring out of her face. "What?" I asked her face.

"Sure. Fine," Orfe said. "Let's."

"What's that face about?"

"I've been waiting for you to suggest it."

Rehearsals grew intensive, not a spectator sport. Yuri and I went to movies if we started to get sent crazy by work or studies or not having much else to do because of the intensive rehearsal schedule. Orfe and the Graces played fewer appearances for a few weeks while they were rehearsing intensively. It happened that two of those were at weddings, and I wonder if that had something to do with Orfe and Yuri deciding they wanted to get married. Orfe didn't ask my advice and didn't listen when I offered it unasked.

The Graces agreed with me, each for a particular reason. Grace Phildon said a person should be clean for at least two years before you committed yourself to him; two years clean gave you a good chance. Willie Grace said she wouldn't want Yuri at her back in a fight, or at her side, or on her side, because she'd just end up trying to take care of him. Raygrace said why fuss around with something that was working just fine, why worry about marriage, it was being good for each other, being good together that mattered.

Orfe ignored all of us. Yuri ignored all of us. We were all more than a little high on ourselves, so maybe they were wise to dismiss us. When I got a phone call offering Orfe and the Graces the chance to go on tour as warm-up band, I wasn't surprised. I passed the information on to Orfe, who turned the job down without hesitation. I wasn't surprised at that either, and I had my objections ready. The Graces weren't saying anything.

"But Orfe," I said.

"They smash up their instruments."

"Those aren't their real ones. You know that."

"But that's even worse. You know I'm right."

"No, I don't," I said. "I know you got your start,

your real start, vomiting all over the stage." I don't know why I thought Orfe and the Graces had to go on that tour. Even at that time I knew that the group—if they became anything—would become music history. But I wanted them to do that tour, and maybe I do know why.

"You're not going to be able to talk me into it," Orfe said.

"I told him that."

"Did you, really?"

I hadn't. I had been breathless, excited, bamboozled. I'd been a jerk letting him snow me with his big-name band.

"Good," Orfe said. "Now you can say all the nasty things you want to say, which if you'd refused right away you wouldn't have thought of. Isn't that right?"

"I'm sorry, Orfe," I said, meaning sorry for not being better than I am.

"You realize what it means, this offer?" Orfe asked.

I realized. All of us realized. There was good reason to feel high on ourselves.

▲▲▲▲▲

I walked before Orfe and Yuri at their wedding, and the Graces followed behind. The wedding was held in the park. Vows were exchanged and the guests celebrated the occasion with food and drink, song and dance. That was the first time I heard the Graces play without Orfe, heard Orfe's songs performed without her voice. I remember listening to the Graces doing one of *Yuri's Dreams*, and my then-new boyfriend Michael had his arm around me, keeping me gently close—the song made you want to go somewhere private and make generous love, but you didn't because you wanted to stay to hear the song. You wanted to stay for the whole wedding. That's the kind of wedding Orfe and Yuri had. Until almost the end it was everything a wedding is supposed to be. It was almost the perfect wedding.

When Yuri wandered off with the people from the house, and we figured out where he must have gone, and Orfe went off after him and came back without him, everything changed. After that, after sorrow, there was only the last dance Orfe and the Graces played together. And after that there were only the Graces. Who, starting from their first album, for which they kept Orfe's name, *Yuri's Dreams*, have moved right into the spotlight. The Graces are music history.

THREE

While Jack and the rest of the Jackets accepted applause and admiration, Orfe sat the edge of the platform. She wasn't sitting exactly; she was more wrapped around her own stomach, to comfort it; she was mostly waiting. For the room, and her head, to clear enough so she could get out of there.

She sensed more than saw his approach and heard him begin whatever he'd planned to say, "I'm Smiley's friend—"

Her head snapped up and she was answering, before she thought, "If you're his friend, you ought to tell him he's drugging the talent out of his hands. Out of his arms. Shooting down the drummer he could be if he wasn't shooting up."

The taste of her own vomit was still in her mouth, she told me.

Then she saw who she was talking to. Saw his dark, curly hair, the broad forehead and almost pointed chin, the dark eyes looking into hers. Saw the skin, pale under a sheen of sweat. Saw his hands jammed into his jeans, clenched. Saw what he had done to himself, was doing.

It took a couple of seconds for his response to sink in, as if his words fell into her ears and got temporarily lost in the auricular tubes so it took them a while to get to her brain. "Smiley doesn't shoot."

"You know what I mean," she said, still trying to take him all in, not paying much attention to what she was saying. Feeling bad enough to weep, looking at him, feeling joy.

"Yeah," he said. "I do. I know exactly what you mean. I really hear you." He knew, he told me, that she couldn't understand what he was hoping she had just given him, which she couldn't have given him unless he understood her perfectly, as she, he hoped, would understand him. Wanting so badly for her to understand, he repeated himself. "I hear you loud. I hear you clear."

Orfe lowered her legs, until her feet touched the floor, and stood up. She saw that he was tall, tall and skinny. Tall and skinny and strung out. It made her sad and sick. He saw all of that, although all he really saw, he said, was someone like a flame, and not just her hair, a flame like fire to burn you clean. He'd seen women like that before, he said, he'd seen women of all kinds in plenty, but never one that scorched him. Orfe scorched him.

He lived in the house where Smiley lived, so he could ask Smiley what her name was, where she lived.

If she had a guy. Or anything.

Smiley was pretty fried, but he remembered the street

where Orfe played. Yuri got out of the house then, because he knew what would happen if he stayed, got out and walked away what was left of the night, walked the sun up into the sky, walked away the morning, until around lunchtime he was waiting for her on the street.

He was pretty sure she didn't see him.

He was wrong. Orfe saw him right away, standing in the doorway behind a moving throng of bodies, looking—if it was possible—worse than he had the night before. There was more gray in his pale skin or maybe green; his jeans and shirt looked like he hadn't taken them off to go to bed; his hair curled lank down his neck. She didn't much notice him or think about him, however; she had work to do.

He was still there when she had finished, pocketed the money, and put the guitar away. He stepped out of the doorway and came toward her. She wasn't surprised. "You look like shit," Orfe said.

"I feel about the same," he said. "Are you hungry? I think I want some herbal tea—ginseng or something like that—but a place that has teas probably has food if you're hungry, if you know any place. D'you know a place?" He knew he was having trouble making sense. He couldn't braid his ideas right, as if he held all these different colors and thicknesses in clumsy fingers and he couldn't get his fingers working right. He couldn't get his mind and mouth working right. He didn't want to scare her off.

Orfe wasn't scared, although it crossed her mind. She knew a place and they walked the blocks over to it, not saying much. What's your name? they said, and Where did you grow up? and What are you doing here in the city, now?

Yuri ordered a pot of tea. He gulped down the first cup blistering hot, and that perked him up. "I don't want you to think I'm crazy," he said.

Orfe shook her head, she didn't. "Drugged out," she said.

"Yeah. I know. I'm—" He didn't want to make any promises to her, because they might turn out to be false. Not trustworthy, that was what drugs made you into. So no promises. "Listen," he said, "when you—"

He saw how she swung her face away at the words, as if she knew what he was going to name and was ashamed. He reached across to hold her chin and turn her face back to him—

The softness of her skin, and the line of bone along her jaw, under the skin . . . He thought she must feel his hand shaking.

"Listen. It's as if—you do it *for* me. Get the poison out of me when you—I can't do it for myself, I can only want to and wish I could, I can only feel like it and that's the only feeling I have unless I can keep all that shit locked out. You know how I lock it out?"

Orfe nodded her head. He took his hand away.

"I'm going into detox," he said, promising. "I haven't—Since last night, the last time was before I saw you. Everything's changed. You've changed everything."

"How could I?"

"I can't think, you know? It's not—my head's not—I was listening to you and I was okay." He poured out another cup of tea. "I really liked that one," he said, and he stumbled through a couple of lines of a song. "That one. You know?"

"Of course I know. I sang it."

"Made me feel like a kid again," Yuri said, and he looked like a happy little kid to her, for just a couple of seconds, for just a glimpse.

"I wrote it," she said.

"No kidding? Then you're really good, aren't you?" he asked as if it didn't surprise him in the least. As if it was the most natural thing. As if it was the way things ought to be. "That one's the best. Except for 'It Makes Me Sick,' but you didn't write that one, did you? I didn't think so."

"How come?"

He shrugged; it wasn't something he could explain. "But you ought to know, when it makes you sick—you know?"

Orfe looked down, hiding her face.

"You speak for all of us," Yuri said.

Orfe could feel the anger in her eyes. Yuri pulled back from it, then leaned forward into it, toward her.

"I throw up for all of you," Orfe corrected him.

"I didn't think about it that way," he said, "I just—grateful, somebody understood. That's all I thought of."

"For all of us," Orfe said.

"I don't blame you for hating it," Yuri said.

He didn't blame her for doing it either. Of all the reactions, his was the first that touched her own.

"I don't think I ever want to see you doing that again," Yuri said. "When you feel that way about it."

For the first time Orfe thought she might leave Jack and the Jackets sooner rather than later. Soon, in fact.

"Thank you," she said.

"Well, okay," he said. He was watching her, just watching. She felt, under the look in his dark brown eyes, the way the ground feels in spring, when the sun falls on it. She told me later, "He had sunlight in his eyes. I know, it sounds dippy." It didn't sound dippy to me.

"Well, I wish," Yuri said. "Like, if I could tuck you into my ear."

"You'd have to miniaturize me."

"Like *Honey, I Shrunk the Kids*."

"Like Racquel Welch in *Fantastic Voyage*. I won't do it if I can't be like Racquel Welch." Orfe was laughing.

"I'd just tuck you into my ear and take you along with me." Yuri didn't even feel that bad, right then, with Orfe laughing and the hot tea and hope.

"That's not much of a life, down inside someone's ear," Orfe said. "Think about it. If it was actual, it wouldn't be any too pleasant."

"You could say I'm living in someone's ear right now. If you say that, you know how it is for me. And I think I better go now."

Orfe nodded. Sitting there. Watching Yuri's face, and his hands pull out a wad of money from his pocket to drop some onto the table.

"But you wouldn't give me something? Like that sweater? Just to take with me. Keep with me."

"It's not mine."

"Well," Yuri said, standing beside the table now, hands dangling at his side, knowing it shouldn't matter so much about a sweater, if she would let him take it, if it belonged to someone else.

"I borrowed it from a friend," Orfe said.

"An old friend?" Yuri didn't know what she was telling him, and he didn't want to know, if it was going to turn out to be something he didn't want to know.

"An old friend since I was a kid. Since grade school."

"Oh." If he asked and she gave the wrong answer, he didn't know what he would do. He thought he shouldn't ask and decided not to. He could find out later, after. But what difference would it make to learn the worst right now? He asked. "A boyfriend?"

"No. I guess Enny won't mind about her sweater if I tell her why."

"Well. What will you tell her?"

"I'll tell her you liked my singing, my songs. She likes them too. She always did. Always—"

But he was gone by then, out the door and onto the street, the sweater in his hands, sweat oozing down the back of his neck, down the inside of his thighs. Orfe didn't try to follow him. She didn't know if she'd ever see him, or my sweater, again.

▲▲▲▲▲

Yuri never talked about his time in detox and rehab.

▲▲▲▲▲

When the steel door closed behind Yuri, and he stood on the sidewalk under a gritty gray sky, he had a couple of addresses in his pocket for places to go next, where he could find a room with people who knew what he'd already faced and what he faced next; and who might be able to steer him to a job he could do well enough to keep it. He felt shaky, he said, and he thought he probably looked shaky too. Except not as shaky as he had weeks ago when he went in through that same steel door.

The first thing he did was go back to the Atomic Café. Jack and the Jackets were no longer playing there, so he went to the house. He wouldn't go inside, although he thought he could have and been all right. He didn't go inside because he didn't want to risk it, not in the smallest way. He said he knew it was the risk of being lost, entirely, and lost forever.

So he stayed on the stoop even though it was drizzling rain and he didn't have a hat. Smiley stayed under cover in the open door, propped up against the door frame, his hands moving constantly to pockets, chest, behind him, his fingers playing against the wooden frame, not really looking at Yuri. "We've got some good stuff in here. You're looking cool, man. C'mon in, don't be a stranger."

"Where are you playing now?" At the expression on Smiley's face he specified, "Jack and the Jackets, if I want to hear you, where do I go these days? Orfe," he said.

"At the Ivry Gate sometimes," Smiley said. His left hand played along the edges of his T-shirt. "When there's no one they like better they can get."

Yuri nodded. "Thanks, man."

"But I'm not playing with Jack anymore."

"Who're you playing with?"

"I'm looking for a new group. I heard of someone, I've got to check it out, it'll be cool, I think. Lotsa money. Lotsa good stuff.

Yuri nodded. "Luck, man." But Smiley needed, he said, more than luck; it would take a miracle now, for Smiley. Behind Smiley, the house sat waiting like a death trap, its mouth open, to eat you alive.

"Orfe neither," Smiley said. His right hand flew up to his face. "I thought you'd pay attention to that. She quit, Jack chewed nails for a while, it pissed me off too. I don't know where she is; she hangs out with that friend of hers."

"What friend?" Yuri didn't know anything about Orfe.

"The college kid. They're trying to get a band together, I heard, but she didn't look like she knew anything about music. The college kid. Orfe's got some funny friends, if you ask me. I dunno, Yuri, it doesn't seem like she treated the rest of us right; does it seem that way to you?"

Yuri shrugged. He wouldn't want to work with Smiley. But Smiley was so far gone it wouldn't do him any good to be told that. And if he'd been reasonably clean, it would just break his heart. The truth wasn't exactly good news. The truth wasn't exactly the kind of thing that made you sit up and start singing. Yuri didn't want to waste his breath on Smiley, and he didn't want to hurt Smiley, so he didn't say anything. "See you. Sometime."

"Yeah, around, man."

Smiley would have forgotten Yuri by the time the door closed, that was what Yuri thought, before he'd gotten halfway down the hall, that was Yuri's bet.

Yuri took Smiley's news for a slow-down signal and went to one of the rooming house addresses he'd been given. He unpacked the underwear and shirts from his knapsack into a bureau. The room was small, but it was his. The couple who owned the boardinghouse seemed okay, aware but not judgy. His life was getting back into a better direction. He got himself hired to clerk in a hardware store a couple of blocks away, the first of the places he asked at. He happened to ask, they happened to need someone, problem solved. He signed himself up for a couple of the outreach education courses that were offered free in the evenings, Beginning Accounting and Intro Biology, the first because he thought it would be useful to know and the second because he thought he ought to understand himself better.

"Getting ready, I was the get-ready man, in get-ready mode," he told me. "And making sure I could stay clean, keep myself clean. Making sure I'd be safe in my own hands. Otherwise, how would she be, you know?"

He set up a schedule and kept to it. He went to classes, NA meetings, went to work, did homework, saved part of each paycheck. He didn't go back to see old friends, "if you could call them that." He felt flaky a lot of the time, "but that eased up too."

He did no more than keep an eye out for Orfe. He knew he'd find her, sooner or later, and he wanted it to be sooner but was more afraid of finding her too soon than too late. It didn't take him long to hear where she was living—with me. That was just a matter of asking questions in a cafeteria, outside a library, on a street corner. He could have walked up to her anytime, it wasn't that he couldn't find her.

It wasn't that he didn't know what to do with a girl either. There had always been girls for Yuri. He'd always been there for the girls too. Some lasted awhile, some lasted an evening, all of them he said he loved and meant it. Girls, women, females—he thought they were wonderful, the way they thought and the way they smelled and the way they were smoothly curved, the way they could cry, the way they had a whole variety of emotions and their ideas and their senses of humor and not one of them ever the same as any one of the rest of them. It wasn't that Yuri didn't know what love was. He'd had a lot of experience of love, falling into it, falling out of it, fending it off, gathering it in. In fact, he said, that was the trouble. He'd had so much experience that he couldn't help but know that this time he was in a different league. In this league he still knew everything he knew, but he didn't know anything compared to what he needed to know.

There was never any question: Yuri was for Orfe, Orfe for Yuri. When he finally approached the street where she was playing, she saw him right away. Her fingers stumbled on the guitar, just an instant's stutter.

Her voice didn't lose its place or melody—it just rang like a bell that has finally been struck true. Yuri waited until she was finished performing and had gathered up the money and had closed away the guitar. He didn't even try to touch her.

Because Orfe had no idea. That's what he hadn't known until he saw her, saw her face and heard her voice when she knew he was there, watching her. He knew he was going to have to let her teach him what she didn't even know she knew.

All of this thinking and knowing was going on underneath, all of this trying to understand—or at least trying to be sure he wasn't misunderstanding everything—all of it was going on deep inside him. On the outside he was seeing her and going up to her, saying hi, asking if he could buy her something to eat and trying to hear her answer at the same time that he could barely breathe when her eyes looked right into his eyes, asking her if she'd like to take a walk but not saying—yet—where to, at the same time he was noticing that her wrists were stronger-looking than he'd remembered and being sure he told her he was drying the sweater, after hand washing it, so she'd know he was a responsible person and promising her he'd give it to her when it was dry so she'd know he planned to keep on seeing her. Trying to read her expression so he'd be sure she wanted to see *him* again. Inhaling the clean and clear smell of her and the sense of her standing close to him. Wondering what might happen. Jittery on the edge of lust. He was about to start getting to know her, and his brain almost supernovaed with it.

He'd never felt so alive, Yuri said. Being high was nothing compared to this. He felt like he'd been split open and was just lying there, while everything in the world poured into him, and he was holding the sides of himself open like a flasher's coat to let it all pour in. He'd never known how roomy he was, inside.

If there was something you could buy and take, anything like this, Yuri said, it would blow the top of your head off. Everybody who took it would just die of it all the time.

Orfe had a sandwich with him, he carried her guitar, and they walked, talking all the time. He walked her around his life, apartment buildings, and schools—grade school, middle school, high school, the community college campus where he'd gone for three months before dropping out because he needed the money and the time for drugs. The steel door and brick building and high-fenced grounds of the rehab center. Movies, Christmases, teachers, friends, pets, thoughts about heavy metal and the homeless, government, God, dances, wars, pizzas, Lennon—they got as much told as they could. They sat around in the kitchen of his rooming house for the long dark hours of that first night, talking. When Orfe said it was time for her to get some sleep, Yuri walked her back to the dormitory, and they spent the early morning hours talking in the common room, each curled up in a chair.

Yuri did most of the talking. Orfe mostly listened. He figured out almost immediately that the most of what went on in her, what was most important to her or cut her most deeply, got told about in her music. So he didn't ask her to tell him all that much, and he didn't feel bad about doing so much talking.

It was a weekend, Yuri said, and that was lucky because he finally keeled over around Sunday evening. Orfe had a practice session and he knew better than to ask if he could listen in. "I always knew better," he said, "and I could always do better. With her. It wasn't even a choice, I just did it, it was what I wanted to do, there wasn't anything else I wanted to do, except better. There isn't. Never will be. It's so great. . . ."

Yuri never pressed the word *love* on Orfe. Telling her his feelings didn't matter, telling her his desires or her attractions. He didn't even kiss her until he knew that was what she wanted to do, which he knew without her asking. Kissing her, he said, wasn't like the first move to get her to bed; in itself it was enough. Not that he didn't want her in bed, but—everything about Orfe was enough, and more than enough, in itself. There didn't need to be more. There was more, but that wasn't what mattered. What mattered was what was there, at the time, at any given time.

Yuri had dark hair, tightly curled and worn longish. The curls hung like the tendrils of grape vines. His eyelashes were thick and dark. Yuri had a way of looking right at you, right into your eyes, when he talked to you, as if he didn't want to miss anything about you. He moved tall, loose. Sitting, he relaxed into curves. His clothes smelled faintly of tobacco, and he was always lighting up, blowing smoke, a habit he picked up in rehab. "Otherwise you might go nuts," he said, "or I thought I might, which is about the same thing." Yuri danced tirelessly, alone or with a partner or in a circle. He played soccer in the park—a swooping wing. He liked ocean swimming and cooking—Chinese was his specialty, and soups.

Yuri was the kind of guy who, when he'd made you a dinner and the two of you had washed dishes afterward and dried them and put them away, would remember to scour out the sink and sweep the floor. He liked to work and talk. If you wanted to stay on at the store after it closed Saturday noon and sort the sales slips and pass them to Yuri so he could enter totals into a calculator, that was great with him, or if you wanted to sit and watch him play in a pickup soccer game, that was fine too. But he'd call out French vocabulary words for you too, or help you sort out index cards for a research paper or talk about the effects of different corporate structures on middle management morale.

The only thing Yuri wasn't was ambitious, and, as he said, Orfe was ambitious enough for both of them and all their children too. "I plan to be able to be self-sufficient," Yuri said to me, "but that doesn't mean I have to *be* that. It's enough for me that I don't *have* to be dependent. If you get me. Yeah, you get me, you know exactly what I mean, you're good at knowing what people mean—however badly they might say it. Aren't you? C'mon, Enny, you can admit to me what you really know about yourself."

If Yuri chose you to love, you knew he could love

you more than anybody else would. To win his love would be the best thing that could happen to you. You would love him more than you could anyone else, and better, the best. Yuri would never leave in your mouth the stale taste other old loves had left, going bad, drying up, giving way.

Yuri could have had anybody, and he picked Orfe. Once he picked her, there was nobody else for him. "It's the only thing that makes sense in the world, she is. Y'know? I mean, if there isn't Orfe—for me to love—then I can't handle the world, or anything, and I don't even want to. But there is and I do and I do, so everything's okay. In fact, everything's great. Can you stand it? Yeah, you're tough enough for happiness."

Of course I wanted Yuri. I named my desire what it was, right from the first. But I never wanted to take Yuri away from Orfe, I would never have wished Orfe the grief of losing Yuri. So that, while I wanted him, I didn't hope he would want me. I learned about love from Yuri.

▲▲▲▲▲

It took a while for Orfe to understand, to figure out the truth, as she put it. At first she thought Yuri was a friend. A better friend than most, a really good friend, the kind of friend who—when they were together both of them were more able to be who they really were, each was more able. "Like you, Enny," she told me.

It took her a while to figure out the truth about Yuri.

He was different from every other friend she had ever had, she learned that. She didn't know if he started out different or got that way, growing slowly into it hour by hour of the time they spent together.

They did what friends do, either just the two of them or in a group. They hung around together. They told the stories of things that happened that day, explained ideas, argued, asked questions, found out the kinds of things you have to hang around together to find out. Who always crosses with the lights, for example. Who finds and gives presents. Who likes peanut butter cups. Who worries about dolphins. Who worries about the Middle East.

They spent hours in the living room of Yuri's boardinghouse, watching old horror movies on late night TV, eating popcorn, and drinking apple juice. Orfe hung around while Yuri gradually cut down on cigarettes—down to two packs a day, a pack and a half, a pack; down to ten, nine, eight—until he'd broken the habit. She liked it that he wouldn't deny that he liked the taste of tobacco. And she liked his way of mismatching his high-topped sneakers, pairing red and black, purple and green, black and purple, red and green. She liked the way he ended up eating three quarters of a pizza they had ordered to split between the two of them, picking the olives off when he moved over onto her half. Yuri almost never said anything about her music, but when she played he always listened. Intently.

It was her songs that told Orfe what she should, she said, have known all along. When she started writing *Yuri's Dreams*, she said, she started to suspect what the truth had been all along. What the truth had to have been all along, or she could never have written those songs.

She didn't know if she could ask him to kiss her (and she wrote a song). She thought that if she didn't find out, she would waste away with wondering (and she wrote a song). She thought that if she found out what she didn't want to know, she would drown in grief (and she wrote a song). Until finally she asked him, "What do you think it means that there's nothing that doesn't get turned into a song, into music, inside me?" and he told her, "You do love me, if that's what's worrying you. And I love you, if you're wondering—there's no question about that."

Once she knew she loved him, Orfe said, she felt that she knew what was going on. It made sense. So that was that.

For a while. For a while they went on in the old way, just with new knowledge. For a while they continued hanging around together, just the two of them or in a group, whenever they could. Orfe couldn't go to work with Yuri, he couldn't go onstage with her; unless she slept on the living room sofa at his rooming house (which she did more and more often, it being more and more often too much trouble to return to my dormitory), they were apart for the sleeping hours. Otherwise they were together. They were as close as any lovers except that, for a while, they weren't lovers.

"What do you mean, 'for a while'?" I asked her.

She shrugged, she wasn't sure, it didn't matter.

"No, I mean, days? a week? a month? seven years?"

"Do you want to hear what he did, after a while, or not?" she asked. "You were there, you already know how long, if it matters. I was right there with you."

"Orfe, you were so much in love, nothing anybody said or did could penetrate the—glow. It was great, seriously, but you weren't exactly in communication. If you don't believe me, ask the Graces."

"Do you want to hear?"

I did.

Hungry was Orfe's word for how she felt, at that time, about Yuri, hungry for the tastes of him. But she didn't dare, because Yuri seemed to talk a lot about what a high love could be, even without sex, without the sensual stuff, an incredible high. "First the spirit," he said to her, "then the flesh. There's a sequence." Orfe nodded her head and poured herself another glass of juice or popped herself another bowl of popcorn; she didn't want to rush at him, and she didn't want to take any part of it away from him, and besides, he knew more about love than she did. "I wouldn't want him telling me to hurry up with music," she said. "So listen to what he did."

What Yuri did was save up enough money to take the two of them away to the beach for a week together, alone. He rented a little house; he asked Orfe to take the week away from her work and she agreed; they took the train out together, a single suitcase between them. What Yuri did was give Orfe a week at the ocean's edge, just the two of them alone together, with nothing but loving to do.

▲▲▲▲▲

When they found an apartment they liked and could afford, they rented it—a one-room-with-sleeping-alcove apartment, across from the park. They furnished it with a mattress, pillows to sit on, a small kitchen table and two stools, a couple of lamps, a couple of Indian madras bedspreads for curtains, a few posters for the walls. They were lovers, living together. Yuri went to work and came home, sometimes to cook and clean, sometimes just to change shoes before going out to watch a rehearsal or a performance. Orfe wrote her songs and rehearsed them at the studio, played gigs, played the streets when they needed money, and came home, sometimes to cook and clean, sometimes just to wait for Yuri to get home.

One night we were all sitting around the apartment, eating Chinese take-out on plastic plates from the Goodwill store, with Vivaldi on the boom box. We all used chopsticks, with varying degrees of skill—except for my boyfriend of the time, whose name was Tommy. Tommy ate with a fork. He probably got more to eat than the rest of us, because we were pretty clumsy with chopsticks, except for Yuri, who handled them adeptly. Yuri was the one who had taught us how to hold the two narrow pieces of wood and how to manipulate them so we could pick up chunks of food.

The dinner was set out on the floor in its carryout boxes: fried dumplings with dipping sauce, spareribs, rice, chicken with cashews, tofu sautéed with vegetables, pork with broccoli. We spooned food onto our plates and then sat on the floor to eat, hunched over, plate in one hand and chopsticks in the other—except for Tommy, who had a fork in one hand. We talked—about Dylan and Morrison, about Charlie Chaplin and Charlie Chan and "Charlie's Angels," about one thing and another, until Yuri said, "I want to marry Orfe."

Orfe didn't say anything.

"Well, hey, congratulations, Orfe," Tommy said.

Orfe was watching her chopsticks as they chased down a cashew. Her face was hidden.

"What does Orfe want?" Grace Phildon asked.

"Dunno. I just asked her," Yuri said.

"You mean, just now?" Raygrace demanded. "You mean, what we heard, that just now, is you asking her to marry you? That's your proposal? What kind of a nut are you?"

"I just thought of it, because this feels so right," Yuri said. His brown eyes were surprised. "Was this the wrong time, Orfe?"

Orfe looked up then and you could see how much she loved him. "It's not bad timing," she said.

"Why would you want to get married?" Tommy asked. "Unless she's pregnant?"

Willie Grace rolled her eyes at me. I laughed. Tommy glared at me. I glared right back at him.

"I didn't say I wanted to get married," Yuri said. He reached out his chopsticks and picked up a dumpling, as easily as if the chopsticks were his fingers. He dipped it into the sauce and then ate half in a single bite. He dipped, then ate the second half. "I said I want to marry Orfe."

"Big difference," Tommy said, sarcastic.

"Yes, it is," Yuri agreed. "Don't *you* want to get married?"

"Of course not," Tommy said. He turned to me as if I had accused him of something. "You knew that," he said.

I rolled my eyes at Willie Grace.

"You plan to get married eventually, don't you?" Yuri asked.

"Well, sure. Have kids, a family, all that. When the time's right. Later."

"Later?"

"Yeah, when I'm settled into the right job, the right life-style, the right woman."

"That's how I feel, except simpler," Yuri said. "All I want is the right woman, and Orfe's her."

"But you're too young. You can't be much over twenty-one—or maybe closer to twenty-five? How old are you, eighteen? Never mind, that doesn't matter, the point is that you're young, you're going to change." Tommy jabbed his fork at Yuri to underline his point. "And who you love is going to change too."

There was a silence in the room.

"Sorry, Orfe," Tommy said. "I didn't mean it personally."

She kept her head bent down, hiding her face.

"But it's true. Everybody knows how unreliable love is, you see somebody and you like her looks and *boom*—what we call chemistry. Freud called it the sex drive, you know, the drive to reproduce. Reproduce the species, that's what he meant. That's all love is."

Across from Tommy, Orfe and Yuri sat on the floor. They weren't even touching except barely their knees, and they weren't even looking at each other; but they proved that everything that Tommy was saying was inadequate.

"I think," I said, figuring that since I'd introduced Tommy to the occasion I ought to see that he didn't ruin it for everyone else, "people fall in love because they don't want to be alone. I don't think it's about reproductive urges. I think it's about loneliness."

Grace Phildon said, "Except, love can be about the loneliest place to be."

"But that's not what you think about when you fall in love, is it?" I pointed out.

"I don't recall thinking about anything," she said, smiling. "I recall a real shortage of thinking. Lots of kissing."

"Followed by morning sickness," Willie Grace said, "followed by a baby that could cry all by itself and dirty its diapers all by itself, followed by—surprise, surprise—the other half of the bed being empty. *Non ocupado*, he having vamoosed."

"That's better than having him stick around getting uglier and uglier on account of his life being ruined and it all being my fault," Grace Phildon answered.

"Better than being married," Tommy echoed, his point proven.

"I sometimes wonder," Raygrace said and then, "Oops, sorry," as a piece of tofu fell onto the floor. He picked it up, still with chopsticks, and scuffed on his knees over to the wastebasket. He dropped it into the wastebasket and returned to the circle, still on his knees. He smiled around at everyone.

"Well? Wonder what? What is it you sometimes wonder?" Willie Grace demanded. "You started to say something."

"Oh. Just that there are different kinds of love. Platonic love, romantic love, erotic love."

"Can you add marital love to that? From Mars, god of offensive warfare," Willie Grace said. "A joke," she explained. When she and Raygrace had combined households, he had brought a couple of boxes of books with him. She was reading away like crazy, she said; they couldn't afford a TV, and with her rehearsal schedule she couldn't manage a relationship, and he was studying all the time he wasn't playing music. So what else was there for her to do but read his books?

"Since it's power that women look for in a man," Tommy said, "getting married young is dumb. Young men have no power, nothing real—not even star athletes, with futures in the professionals." Tommy played football. "Everyone knows power's what women want. What turns them on."

"And here I thought it was money I was after," Grace Phildon laughed.

"Money's power," Tommy said impatiently.

"Everybody's full of crap, as usual," Willie Grace said, looking at me and Tommy. "You don't have any power, so why does she love you?"

"I don't," I said. "You knew that," I told him. He was looking tight around the mouth and harried around the eyes. I knew part of what was bothering him. He'd been looking forward to a once-only evening, with rockers or punks or Deadheads; probably he'd hoped for an orgy. Something he could impress his friends with. "Nobody knows anything about love," I decided.

"I do," Raygrace said. When we stopped laughing at him, he kept on insisting, "I do. Love is when you really want to give to someone else, give feelings and thoughts, help, pleasure, all of it, everything you can," he said. His round cheeks flushed, but he held his ground.

"What does that have to do with marriage?" Tommy demanded.

"Giving is as selfish as any other pleasure," Willie Grace argued, ignoring Tommy's question. "You give to make yourself feel good. The point is that love is selfish, and if you don't know that, you don't know anything."

"Everything gets easier when you love someone," Grace Phildon said.

"No, everything gets harder, because you care so much," Raygrace argued.

"That still doesn't prove what love has to do with marriage," Tommy insisted.

"I want to marry Orfe," Yuri said, "and that's what love has to do with marriage for me. It doesn't matter, though, if you don't want to," he said to Orfe.

"No, I wouldn't mind, if you want to," she said.

For a long second it was as if the rest of us were invisible, the way they looked at one another. I didn't know how I felt, watching that look; I felt uncomfortable, and I wanted to get away. It was too perfect to stay in the same room with, although also it was so perfect that I never wanted to have to leave.

"It'll be great," Yuri said, drawing us all in with his smile. "It'll be the best time anyone has ever had, we'll invite everybody."

"And we'll be the music," Grace Phildon said.

"I'll sing," Orfe said.

"No you won't, you'll be getting married," Raygrace reminded her. "We'll walk you down the aisle with *Yuri's Dreams*, and back up the aisle with *Yuri's Dreams*."

"A church?" Orfe asked. "You didn't say a church. I was thinking the park."

"It doesn't matter," Yuri said.

"I just want to know what you want," Orfe said.

"We're going," Tommy said, and he looked at his watch. He waited for me to scramble up beside him. "Thanks for the dinner, Orfe, Yuri. Nice place you've got here. Good luck with the wedding. Are you ready?" he asked me.

I put our plates and chopsticks and fork into the sink. We left the apartment.

Out on the street he reached for my hand. "You've got some wacko friends."

I had both my hands in my pockets and walked along.

"I mean—that's no time to propose. A proposal's supposed to be private. Just for starters. And then it got so—Jesus, emotional—deep thought, that pseudophilosophy. It was all so sweet my teeth started to hurt."

"You don't like emotions, do you? They make you squirm, don't they?"

"Don't get on my back just because you're jealous."

"Jealous? Of you?"

"How dumb do you think I am, Enny? It's her you're

jealous of. Orfe. Because of him. Yuri. Oh, I've seen you, the way you sometimes look at him. You want him for yourself."

I stopped, lamplight on my face and on Tommy's face. It didn't matter that he was about a foot taller than I was. I felt as if I could punch him senseless and as if I were about to do that. Starting with his cute little nose. "You call that jealous?"

"Come off it." He laughed, more confident now that the odds were even or weighted in his favor.

I said what I said next more bluntly than I might have, because I was disappointed, in myself more than in him. "*You* come off it," I said. "I think I'll say good-bye here."

He wasn't so thick as not to know what I meant. He thought for a minute, anger and chagrin mixing with the embarrassment on his face. "Just because I told you the truth about yourself? Just because I saw through you?"

"Because you saw into me and thought you were seeing through me," I said.

Which was the end of that. I turned around and walked away, back to the apartment. When I opened the door they were busy talking about the wedding, when and where, what kind of ceremony, what to eat. I took my plate and chopsticks out of the sink and sat down to join in.

▲▲▲▲▲

When Orfe was grieving over Yuri, she reminded me of that evening. "I always meant to say how glad I was when you broke up with Tommy," she said. "I like Michael," she told me. "I'd like it if you fell in love with Michael."

I already had.

"I think," Orfe said, "that love is like being alive, in this respect, or peace too. Yeah, all three of them have the quality of—you never feel as if there has been enough. You never say, okay, that's my fair share, that's good enough for me. You always say, More. More, please. I want more, I need—there's never enough, that's what I mean, that's what I think. You get to the end, I—"

Here Orfe stopped speaking for a minute, lowered her face, and then raised it to look out with sorrow like tears but without them, and the worse for that.

"I got to the end and I don't feel like it's been enough. Love. Even though I know it's fair, that love for any amount of time, however little time—to be deeply loved ever is more than any of us has a right to. I know that. But I feel like I could use more, need—"

And she was gone, following her music, her head bent over the guitar.

FOUR

It's not that I can remember so clearly. I only remember shreds, shards, patches. But what I *can* do is re-create, from these fragments, the memory; and the re-creation becomes memory itself.

On the morning of the day Orfe and Yuri got married, sunlight filled the air. Even the asphalt paths that crisscrossed the park sparkled under the sunlight or shone under shade. Celebrants in their wedding-guest finery brought forward platters and bowls of food, set them on the table, and stepped back to become a crowd. Brightly colored skirts—red, blue, yellow—and brightly colored shirts—purple, green, orange—milled about.

I can see how it looked, see the Graces all in a cluster, turning and waving and smiling. I can see Orfe in the dress we found after hours of searching the used clothing stores, a long-sleeved, long white dress with a broad lacy collar. A crown of white flowers floated in the cloud of her red hair. I can see Yuri in a slightly oversize tuxedo jacket, also found in a used clothing store but requiring fewer hours of searching, and the pleated shirt underneath, stiff with starch, white with bluing. I can see his black broad-brimmed felt hat, with the high curved feather rising from its band. I can almost see myself, leading the wedding pair forward into the center of the circle.

Until I remember how the sounds ceased when Yuri turned to Orfe and Orfe turned to Yuri, I don't remember the sounds. But they were there, conversations and laughter, the wash of wine pouring into paper cups, the clink of fruit punch being served out of a glass punch bowl. Some of the guests were uninvited. They were strangers caught up into the occasion as they were sitting around or walking by; some of those were glad to have the adventure added to their day or grateful for the hour's distraction; a few waited patiently to eat, their eyes not on the wedding couple but on the table of food. It seemed as if everybody must be talking—voices pitched loud and louder, soft velvet voices, gruff, rough voices, piercing nasal voices, high and low voices, musical or flat, pompous or serene, eager, laughing, sarcastic, flirtatious, intent—a babble of sounds that ceased when Orfe turned to Yuri and Yuri turned to Orfe, at the center of the circle.

"I promise myself to you," Orfe said to Yuri, "my heart and all the works of my hands." "I promise myself to you," Yuri said to Orfe, "my heart and all the works of my hands." Orfe held out her hand, and Yuri put a ring onto her finger. Yuri held out his hand, and Orfe put a ring onto his finger. They were married.

They turned around, facing away from each other,

standing back to back, and opened their arms out. The circle moved around them.

It was a song and everyone was singing. The Graces had gone to their instruments. Music filled the sunlit air. We sang the song through and then unclasped hands, to clap in applause for the occasion and the wedding couple and ourselves. Orfe laughed and curtsied low, almost sweeping the ground with her arm. Yuri laughed and swept his hat from his head to bow to the four points of the compass.

The bowls and platters were uncovered. The guests, invited and uninvited, helped themselves to cakes and little cookies, to paper cups of wine or fruit punch.

▲▲▲▲▲

They came in a parade, holding a square metal cake pan overhead, as if it were the platform with the god riding on it. These were the people from the house, and they were too late for the exchange of vows, the ceremony itself, if they had ever intended to be in time for it. Yuri and Orfe had signed the back of the marriage certificate, and the Graces and I had witnessed the signatures, before the little parade ever entered the park and came toward the wedding—cake tin held high, garlands of honeysuckle and ivy hung over their shoulders.

I was with Michael. He and I were serving drinks when they arrived. I ladled out fruit punch and he poured red or white wine. We listened to the music, Orfe and the Graces, and watched the dancers, Yuri with various partners. I had danced with Yuri once myself that day; he danced with every woman there, sometimes just one, sometimes gathering two or three or four around him for the dance. Michael and I watched and sometimes commented. The music wasn't amplified and neither were the voices.

Watching Yuri dance, Michael said, "If I were the jealous type, I'd be jealous of him."

"But you're not."

"Nope. I'm the scientist type. The weedy scientist type. So I'm only almost jealous."

"Not over me, I hope," I said.

"No. Although I could be—"

"If you were the type."

"If I were the type. This is just sort of a general jealousy. I don't even know what it is that he has. Do you?"

"Sort of."

"It's not the usual attraction he has, except for his good looks. I'm not putting him down as unmasculine or anything," Michael said. "Just observing."

"I've never heard you put anybody down."

"What's the point?" Michael asked me. Then, "Who's that? Looks like—I don't know what it looks like. Look."

The people from the house, in a procession, came up to the music. They had long hair and many had bare feet. They wore ragged jeans and belts with studs, black T-shirts, denim vests with studs. Their colors were black and silver or black and steel—like the night sky with safety pins and zippers and studs for their stars. Their eyes were dark and shadowed. Their parti-color hair looked dark, whether it was hennaed, bleached, or blackened, or arose in a crest of green or orange spikes. Twisted vines lay across their shoulders, trailed down their chests and backs, swayed with the dance.

They danced up to Yuri and cut him out from among the women. He became the center of their circling dance. It was a dance of giving, the presentation of the cake they carried, which three women held out to him, then drew back, then offered again, as if it were some ceremony of its own. Among all the milling guests, invited and uninvited, strangers and friends, I don't know if Orfe saw Yuri among the people from the house. I saw them dancing, saw them move gradually to the side, saw a silver knife blade flash, saw a square of cake in Yuri's hands, saw him eating, as they watched, saw him licking the frosting from his fingers and taking the pan into his hands, to become the leader of their procession. The people from the house, with Yuri at their head, moved through the crowd in a long sinewy line, toward where Orfe and the Graces played.

But Yuri turned away and the others followed. They wound among the dancers up to the table behind which Michael and I stood. Yuri meant to set the cake down on the table, I thought, but he misjudged where the edge was and it fell, upside down, onto the grass. I moved to pick it up, but Yuri was faster than I. Only he was clumsy, and the cake was left on the ground, its naked chocolate back exposed. Yuri straightened up and looked at me, and his eyes were darker than I'd ever noticed them because the pupils had expanded; he looked helpless, like a baby, with those darkened eyes. He had a tender lift to the corners of his mouth, and he was looking into my eyes, and I thought he might kiss me—thought it with an eager swelling of the heart, a longing upward—just for a second, before I was afraid he would kiss me, and his eyes filled with water, with tears, and he moved away, along a line of music, and the people from the house followed him. The cake was trampled under their feet, but they didn't notice. I stood holding the empty cake tin and didn't hear it when Michael said my name. Yuri's hat moved into and among the crowd, the bright feather curved and waving.

"I'm sorry," I said to Michael. "I wasn't listening. Dance with me, do you want do dance? Let's be guests for a while. Let's celebrate." I wanted to put my hands on Michael's shoulders and I wanted to feel his warm hands on my back. I wanted to touch Michael's reality.

Later, when most of the guests had gone home, Orfe asked me if I knew where Yuri was. I didn't. I hadn't seen him for a while, I wasn't sure how long. Had he gone to the apartment to go to the bathroom? I suggested.

A while after that, as Michael and I were filling yet another plastic bag with crushed paper cups and empty frozen fruit juice containers, Orfe asked us again. "He isn't at the apartment," she said.

"I haven't seen him since—," Michael started. He stopped to think before he said any more. You could see him, behind round glasses, following the ideas to their logical conclusions, before he would say any more.

"Since he was with that group of—looked like street people, you remember," he said to me.

"What street people? What group?" Orfe asked.

"They brought a cake and Yuri had a piece," Michael said. "Then they all came by the table. He dropped the cake. It was ruined, it was underfoot, stepped on—the cake they'd brought."

"He dropped it on purpose," I said.

"That's what I thought," Michael said.

The Graces were behind Orfe, listening.

"He was sorry," I told Orfe.

"He was dosed," Willie Grace guessed, her voice sharp, harsh.

"You think on purpose?" Raygrace asked her. He held her hand, it looked like tight. Michael gripped my hand and I gripped his. Grace Phildon's fingers were fitted close around Cass's little shoulders.

"Sons of a bitch," Willie Grace said. "Sons of bitches."

"I wouldn't think on purpose," Grace Phildon said. "Or I'd think, not so much on purpose as carelessly, as if it were a joke."

"It can't be a joke for Yuri, for someone like Yuri," Raygrace said, puzzled.

"It's never a joke," Michael announced. "It's chemical, it's a measurable and re-creatable reaction, like a laboratory experiment, it's—putting things into the cells of a body changes the cells. That's no joke."

"Fucking sons of fucking bitches. Sandbagged him."

Orfe stood with her arms hanging down at her sides and her hands empty.

"They don't think, though," Grace Phildon said. "I

don't think they can, anymore. So they don't really *do* it. Whatever it is they do, it's not as if they really did it."

I was the one who was weeping. Orfe stood absolutely still.

"And the victim?" Willie Grace demanded. "What about the victim? The victim is still real. He's still there, what's left of him. It's just, there's nobody responsible."

"All that's real is a victim?" Raygrace said. "Because that means there's no way to prevent it happening again. That means all you can do is try to help the victim out, after. After it's too late."

"As if people were an act of God," Willie Grace said. "Like tornadoes or tidal waves."

"What are we going to do?" Grace Phildon asked.

Orfe shook her head, as if to clear it. "I'm going to go get him."

"It's dark," we told her. "Wait until morning, it's not safe around there. You can't tell how—wait until the stuff has worn off a little," we asked her. "We'll all go," we said.

"No. He won't—you can't," she said. "If you do, he'll never come with me, he'll be too ashamed."

"They'll try to keep you out," Raygrace said.

"He was really sorry," I said to Orfe. She knew what I meant.

"I'm the only who has a chance," she explained to everybody else. "My only chance is alone, if I'm alone. They won't be afraid of me. Yuri won't be afraid."

"Yeah, but what about getting there?" Michael asked.

"What about being there, and also what about getting back?"

Orfe bent her head.

"You can't tell what the shits will do," Willie Grace said. "Be real, you know that's true."

"Irrational behavior is characteristic," Michael agreed. "Unpredictable behavior."

"Even if what they do isn't what they want to do, still, if they *do* it," Raygrace said.

Orfe stood with her head bent.

"Except it is what they do, and if it was Cass there now—," Grace Phildon said.

Orfe raised her face and, just for a second, I could see in her eyes a catch-me-if-you-can expression. I'd seen it before, in games of red rover. It was there for just a second before she had it hidden behind a hand that brushed hair out of her eyes. When she lowered her hand, her eyes were full of resolution and good sense. If you looked at her, if the glance of her eyes fell over you, you would know that she had resolved on sensible action, which was what we'd advised. The Graces relaxed, and Michael relaxed.

I knew better.

I knew better and I didn't blame her: If there is someone like Yuri in your life, the only sensible line of action is to do everything you can to keep him or get him back. Anything else is nonsense. Is cowardice or a failure of love. If you can climb Annapurna, then there is no other mountain you want to set your feet on, no matter how much good sense people talk to you, about how high and hurtful Annapurna is. The only thing that made sense was for Orfe to go to the house and find Yuri. I didn't think Yuri would ever come back on his own, not now that he had failed. When you have failed once, you know you can fail again; until then you can hope you won't. Having failed her once, Yuri would refuse to leave her in a position where she could be failed by him again. Yuri knew how to love.

Orfe looked around at all of us, her eyes pouring out good sense and reliability. Everybody felt better. Cass moved back to do a little jumping dance, a child's private ceremony of happiness. We completed the clearing up and went back to the apartment for a cup of tea, a glass of juice, a brief conversation about what to do next. The Graces and Casss left, with plans to return in the early morning, first light, and maybe with reinforcements since there is safety in numbers and it never hurts to have your friends at your back in case of a fight. Willie Grace made that point. Although, she added, she thought everybody in the house would be too wasted to make a fist by morning.

Michael and I left shortly after. Orfe stood in the door, talking, her bright hair massed above the lacy collar of the wedding dress. Michael and I walked down the narrow staircase and out into the dark street. The park was empty now, and our full garbage bags leaned like the sleeping homeless against the parking meters.

At the corner I stopped walking and put a hand on Michael's arm. His hair, cropped so short you could see the shape of his head, looked star white under the streetlight. His glasses glinted so that I couldn't see his eyes.

Michael put a couple of fingers across my mouth, as if he knew what I was going to say and wanted to prevent me from saying it. "Take care," he asked.

I watched him walk away, down a dark street, and listened to his footsteps, which had faded away before he turned a corner and became invisible. Then I settled down to wait.

▲▲▲▲▲

I have no idea how long it took. The sky didn't grow darker, the stars didn't come out. City lights made it look as if thick yellow-red clouds floated over the back-drop of a night sky. City dwellers moved through the lighted night, in couples, in groups of three, five, ten, and—although more and more rarely as it grew later—solitary walkers. Orfe descended the steps from the apart-ment building. She had changed into jeans and a turtle-neck. Her guitar was slung over her back.

She had changed her shoes too, to sneakers, and I was hard put to keep her in sight in my high-heeled wedding sandals, hard put to move silently. I wasn't successful. It was no more than a block and a half before Orfe stopped, turned impatiently around, and motioned me to hurry up. She didn't say anything. I couldn't think of anything to say.

We didn't talk. I was afraid that if I said anything, it would be the wrong thing and she would ask me to stay behind, ask me urgently in the name of friendship or love or hope, ask me in a way I couldn't refuse.

The streets got darker, dirtier, less inhabited, less

habitable. Knots of people stood around cars under the yellow streetlights, stood around in doorways, stood around on corners. They watched us without curiosity, without interest—flat eyes in expressionless faces. By then I had taken off my shoes and went barefoot. Shoes in your hands might be weapons, with their sharp narrow heels.

The house was one of a row of houses, each with its six-step stoop, each with its broken windows, some of them patched with tape, some boarded over, some bare sharp glass. Orfe went up the steps and I followed her. She pushed the door open.

There was a hallway with closed doors. At the far end there was a little blue light and the sound of voices and the sound of music and moving shadows. Orfe went down the hallway without hesitating. I hesitated.

I heard them greeting her. The music—drums and guitars—broke off, unevenly, then stopped. I heard clapping, whistles, feet stamping. " 'Sick,' 'It Makes Me Sick,' " I heard that requested, and "Satisfaction." "Where's the rest of you?" someone asked, "Are you alone?" " 'Black and Blue.' " "Yeah, that's a good one, do that too." I couldn't see into the room from where I stood, just the long dim hallway and a tall rectangle of light. I pressed myself into the cracked plaster of the wall. I inhaled the smells of the house.

It was like the time I was thirteen and I climbed up the ladder to the high diving board because I thought if I had climbed up, I would have to have the courage to dive off.

I didn't know, if I went down the hall, what I would see or what might happen to me. Orfe had music and she was Yuri's girl. I had no protection.

When I was thirteen I had turned around and climbed back down off the high diving board, and I thought less of myself ever after. So I went down the hallway.

It was a long room, with shades pulled down over the windows and a black-and-white television flickering in a corner. The floor was bare wood, scattered over with sofas, upholstered chairs, pillows, ashtrays, cans of beer and soda, bindles and sneaks, empty wine bottles with candles burning in them, lamps with scarves and sheets draped over them to ease the light. The room was filled with smoke and shadows.

At the far end of the room Orfe was playing. Smiley sat at the drum set behind her, and a couple of others played along—guitar, slide guitar, also plugged into the amplifiers. Orfe was playing and they were trying to follow her lead. She was trying to gather them into a song.

In the darkness around the musicians, some people were dancing. I could see heads, mostly, like cutout silhouettes, and arms sometimes raised up and a flowing of moving bodies. Across the front of the crowd a profile with spiked hair moved back and forth, like some kind of sentry wearing a crested helmet.

More people sprawled around on the floor, hunched over to snort a line or light a smoke, stretched out flat or twined together, in a pair, in a tumble of bodies. " 'It Makes Me Sick,' " a voice called out.

Orfe turned her pale face to the darkness where the voice came from and shook her head and played on, singing.

I saw Yuri at last, leaning back in a deep chair, closed eyes, a tangle of dark hair, and his neck exposed. One girl, bare breasted I thought, although I couldn't be sure, curled up against his pleated wedding shirt. Another rested her head across his thighs, and her arms were wrapped around his legs as she kneeled beside him.

Person by person, Orfe gathered the whole room up into her songs, one by one. Yuri sat up, shook himself free of the girls, wrapped his hands around his knees, opened his eyes. More and more people joined the dancers, dancing. I turned and left. Went down the long hallway with my shoes still in my hands. Sat down on the steps outside to wait.

It was a long time I sat there, waiting on the steps.

Orfe came out alone, the guitar on her back. There was nobody following her. She turned around to pull the door closed behind her. I stood up to go with her.

The streets were hollow, the sky going gray with false dawn. Orfe walked with her head bent, her face hidden. At her own door she turned around and raised her face to me, and her eyes said as clearly as if she had actually spoken the words, *Don't you dare*.

"I won't, I wouldn't," I promised, before I had time to think.

▲▲▲▲▲

Yuri was gone, and then the Graces were gone too, touring as an opening band, without Orfe, who mostly lived at the studio. I mostly lived at the apartment, occasionally returning to my dormitory to pick up books or mail or clothing. The apartment was just about my home for the final semester. I slept in the double bed, ate off the plastic plates, mopped the linoleum floor. I paid the rent and the electric bill and the phone bill. Whenever Orfe showed up for a bath or a meal or a night, I was there to open a can of soup, get out clean towels, move into a sleeping bag on the floor. I watered the plants. I packed up Yuri's clothes and delivered them to the house. I typed out job applications sitting cross-legged on the floor in front of the typewriter. I studied for my final exams, sitting on a stool at the little kitchen table.

The Graces went on the tour because the offer was just too good. They couldn't, they said, stand on pride the way Orfe could. They understood that this wasn't a time for her to do any performing, they didn't expect her to go along. It was only for a few weeks, it wasn't as if the band was breaking up or didn't plan to get back together. Willie Grace and Raygrace weren't even subletting their apartment, here was the key, either Orfe or I could live there, whoever.

I wasn't sure Orfe even heard them, but I thanked them and took the keys, promised to water the plants, feed the fish, promised to visit Cass at her grandmother's, promised to continue being manager, there was no question, I'd go on dealing with job offers and they could keep sending the checks on to me.

I don't remember how long it was before the evening Orfe and I were eating tuna-fish sandwiches, talking about I can't remember what, and there was the sound of a lot of footsteps and then knocking on the apartment door. The Graces had returned, much sooner than expected, carrying pizza in boxes, holding Cass by the hand.

"But—" I held the door open.

They surged past me, sat down on the floor, opened the pizza boxes, and asked for a pizza wheel, and plates, and were there any napkins.

"C'mon. You'd rather have pizza, I can tell by looking at your faces," Raygrace urged. He was right, of course, so Orfe and I abandoned the tuna to sit down among the Graces.

"What about Tulsa?" I asked. "What about Tucumcari? What about Johnstown?"

"We're fired," Grace Phildon explained. She didn't look upset. She didn't look as if she were fresh back from a failure experience.

"How could you be fired? You're three times as good as the headliner," I protested.

"That's it in a nutshell," Raygrace said. He chomped down on a slice of pizza with green peppers, onions, olives, and anchovies.

"They weren't bad," Willie Grace told us. "But we were better. *Much* better. The audiences didn't want us to leave the stage, they'd call to get us back on, we were playing at the start and then at the finish too. So we were fired."

"With full pay," Grace Phildon said. "Also compensation for our disappointment and the loss of exposure time. It couldn't be better, if you ask me."

"Yeah, they really stank," Willie Grace said. "Stink," she poked a tickling finger into Cass's left armpit. Cass giggled. "Stank." She tickled the other armpit and Cass laughed out loud. "Stunk!" she cried and scrabbled at Cass's stomach with five fingers. Cass fell over backward, laughing, pizza held aloft. "I mean," Willie Grace said, "there was this throb-throb-throb stuff, every song, and this pelvis stuff"—she held out her hand and rocked it forward, again and again, like a little five-fingered pelvis. "It was dumb. Rotten music. And the songs." She turned to Orfe. "The songs made 'It Makes Me Sick' sound like opera, like Mozart opera. Maybe three words, that's about the extent of the lyrics they knew, the S-word"—she winked at Cass—"the F-word, the H-word. Over and over, throb-throb, pelvis, pelvis. You get the picture."

"The H-word?" I wondered.

"Hate," Willie Grace said. "If I never hear that word again in all my born days, I'll be grateful."

"I hate liver," Cass volunteered.

"Well, I guess I don't have to worry about being grateful," Willie Grace said.

"And I hate lima beans," Cass said.

"We were terrific," Raygrace said. "Really good and getting better."

"So what's next?" Grace Phildon asked me. "Are you working again?" she asked Orfe. "Anything new for us to try?"

"Or not," Willie Grace said quickly.

"Whatever, we're fine with it," Raygrace said.

Orfe raised her head and looked around at all of us. I couldn't read her eyes, but there was in her face anticipation and sorrow and acceptance and friendship. "I've got a couple of songs. I'd like you to hear them. Do we have any jobs to play?"

"We will as soon as I get on the phone tomorrow morning," I promised them all.

"Allow rehearsal time," Orfe asked me.

▲▲▲▲▲

Orfe and the Graces practiced at the studio and I was busy: job interviews and renting the college gym for a concert; designing and having printed posters, designing and having printed tickets, and more job interviews, some of them second and third rounds; seeing to ticket sales, seeing to lights and circuitry, renting trucks to carry equipment, starting a career-track job, considering the ways to protect the gym floor and finding someone who would—quickly and on short notice should it be necessary—refinish it. An All-Shoes-Barred Concert, that's what we called it, that's how the posters and tickets read. But there is always someone, there are always some people, convinced that the rules don't apply to them, convinced that doing what she wants takes precedence over anyone else's need or weal. To whom rules are always for other people, not for him. So I needed to have that base covered, in case the gym floor was damaged. I also went around to the few contacts I knew of that might prove useful, a couple of scouts, a couple of booking agents, a few media personnel. They might or might not come. I sent or hand delivered complimentary tickets.

I didn't send or hand deliver a ticket to Yuri.

The crowd filled the whole gym, milling about and waiting. Shoes piled up against walls, as more and more people came in through the wide double doors to push the assembled crowd toward the one section of bleachers we'd left standing. That was the stage, the eight ascending bleacher benches on their scaffolded skeleton. I operated the fairly primitive lighting from a small light board on a table beside the doors. The metal box full of ticket stubs and gate money I put under the table.

Amplifiers were set under the bleachers, on the floor, with wires coming out like tentacles to attach to the instruments. The Graces stayed at about the first or second bleacher row, or on the floor right in front if there was a routine they were doing. Orfe moved up around three of the top four rows—the very top row she avoided, because there wasn't enough room there even to turn around, between the narrow seat and the wall. So Orfe, in her black stretch jeans and white poet's shirt, her hair blazing under the lights and her guitar gleaming, moved up and down around three of the four top rows of bleachers, while the Graces flowed back and forth below, careful to be near enough to the standing mikes, careful not to get their cords too tangled up in the intricacies of the dance and the intricacies of the music.

For the first set, they played *Yuri's Dreams*. The music

filled the air of the gym, from wall to wall and up to the high ceilings where fans rotated behind metal grids. "Gray ashes and white bones," they sang, "The Lament of the Lion Lady," a frightening dream, "White bits of bones buried in gray ashes." The audience swayed, and the Graces swayed in the bright lights, while Orfe sang. "Ashes and bones, bones in ashes." Michael put his hand into mine: I remember that. The song not so much brought his hand into mine as it made me aware of his hand in mine. Hands as flesh over bone, long-boned fingers with their ability, in some cases, to call music out of boxes of wood or plastic, out of strands of steel.

"Soar." Orfe sang another Dream, "Icarus," and the Graces echoed and reechoed the word, "up, Air," the song rising, pulling the echoing voices after it, "up, High," like birds flying, the words, like birds flying up into the crown of the sky and breaking free through it, "Swoop." The words were disconnected, there was no sentence, no story, just melody and music and wild words, and my heart rose with the song, as I listened. I couldn't catch my breath, almost; almost I couldn't breathe.

Orfe sang, last in the first set, "The Oak Tree and the Linden," a song that—because it entered my bloodstream and drove around and around my body until my whole being existed only in the song—I called a love song, even though, as I rode it back, riding my own blood back into the heart of music, it never had the word in it. "The sun makes golden windows of the leaves," Orfe sang with the Graces.

When the set was finished, the audience broke out in applause. Michael turned to me, his hands over his ears, dazed by the sound and displeased, amazed by the enthusiasm and amused. I brought up the lights and brought down the spots. Somebody opened the gym doors. People crowded around past us, where we stood behind the light board. I thought about Yuri.

"From the point of view of time, or history," Michael said from close behind me, "or the stars—from the point of view of the whole universe, from the big bang on—we're nothing, us, right now, just like ants, smaller, just particles, quarks—from that point of view, we're just little minuscule moving things."

"So none of it really matters," I agreed.

"I find that a comforting thought," Michael said. "When things matter too much and can't be helped. Yuri, for example."

My eyes filled with tears, for Yuri.

"Did you ever hear of the energy of mass?" Michael asked.

I turned to look into his face. "No. Why?" He would have a reason for the question.

"Every particle has it," he told me. "Anything that has mass, has it. It's not the same as energy of motion. Energy of mass is the energy in $E = mc^2$, it's an incredible amount of energy. Because *c* in the formula is the speed of light. That's one hundred eighty-six thousand miles per second per second."

I nodded, I knew that.

"That's the speed of light squared, then multiplied times mass—imagine the energy. There's enough energy of mass in a quarter to run New York City during rush hour, I read that, in a book. By a man named Goldsmith.

An astrophysicist. So it's reliable data. So you can imagine the energy of mass in a human being."

I tried to see it, envisioning the invisible and immeasurable energy of mass of an atom, a cell, a person; I could almost see it. Seeing it, I asked, "Do you mean a soul? Do you mean a human being might have a soul?"

The second set started out with dance songs, and the shoeless audience moved along the music like waves along the surface of the water. Then Orfe did one of her new songs. The song had no words, only a voice, calling. The song was melody on a rising *oh* sound, maybe what the stars and planets call out to one another across the empty reaches of space, the voices of solitary stars and silent planets crying out. Then Orfe was singing *ah*, and the audience pressed forward, as if she were calling them forward.

I could feel the press in the darkness. I could feel the call from the figure at the top of the bleachers. I could see, in the shadowy darkness beyond the spotlights, the darkness rising to her.

Orfe's head was bent as she sang. I couldn't make sense of the song, of my own feelings: joy and fear and hope; celebration, mourning, grief, despair, and farewell. The music called me into itself. There were no words, and if there had been, I could not have sung them.

The crowd came closer, darker. Orfe called out from the top row of bleachers, with her head bent, and all the dark crowd seemed to wait for what would happen next, as she sang. All the dark crowd seemed unable to wait, and it pressed in.

The instruments the Graces played on seemed to protest, losing their hold on the music.

The Graces and their instruments seemed to be swallowed up.

Orfe lifted her calling voice. She lifted her head and I could have sworn that she saw me. *Don't be afraid.*

Chaos rose up from beneath the spotlights. The bleachers under Orfe collapsed. She fell into them, as if into an open mouth. The Graces were gone, invisible, lost in the shapeless crowd. The instruments and amplifiers and wires couldn't be seen.

I heard cracking and screaming, wood and people.

All music ceased.

It was a chaos of noise and voices, shouts for help, cries for order.

I turned up the lights but couldn't see what had happened behind the shoulders and backs, backs of heads.

I shoved, pushed, elbowed my way forward. The crowd, pulling back now, pulling away and fleeing, tried to take me with it. I didn't know what Orfe meant: *Don't be afraid.* I only knew, trying to hold my place in the receding tide of people between me and where Orfe had sung on the bleachers, what she hadn't meant.

▲▲▲▲▲

What killed Orfe I don't know, and I don't really care. Whether it was the fall or the press of the audience, the lack of somebody who knew how to administer CPR, or a broken heart, makes no difference. I don't know if she was smothered, crushed, hit by falling debris, hit by a single falling board, or drowned by her own blood as it rose up into her lungs; if her spine snapped or her heart stopped or her brain cells burst. We followed the ambulance to the hospital, the Graces and I, we went to the funeral home, following the coffin as far as we were allowed. Then we went on with our lives.

Yuri never did, as far as I know. We called the house to tell him, but he didn't come to the phone. I sent him a newspaper clipping about the accident. Because he is Orfe's husband and heir, the Graces pay into his account her share of royalties for *Yuri's Dreams*, which he still draws on, so I assume Yuri is still safely alive.

▲▲▲▲▲

Raygrace said to me, "You know, just because it doesn't end happily doesn't mean it's not a love story."

"Yeah, well, neither does it mean it is, just because it has a happy ending," Willie Grace snapped back at him.

This was at their wedding, a long time after. Grace Phildon raised her glass of champagne to all of us, Willie Grace and Raygrace, Cass, Michael and me.

I raised my glass in response. "Love stories aren't about how they end," I promised them.

FIVE

"You were with me," Orfe said. "I saw you in the doorway. You didn't come into the room. Or you couldn't. Or you wouldn't."

This was later when she told me this.

"But you were waiting when I came out. And I never said so at the time, but I was glad. I am glad. Having you there. Because I don't know what I would have done without you. Not just then, but especially then, because you were there, you know what it was like, walking into that house. You were great, Enny."

I said, "I was just following you."

"Dark, and it smelled of garbage and dope. Stale urine, stale sweat, stale sex."

"You were the brave one," I said.

"And their voices were all sort of low and monotonous. The way the light was dim and diffused around the whole long room—it was like being underwater, among the drowned. It was like the house of death.

"Yuri told me," she said. "At some point that night he told me what happened. They put dope into the frosting, when they gave him that piece of their wedding cake. By the time we got there they were all wasted, and Yuri was wasted too.

"I played every song I knew and some I hadn't even written until right then. They wanted 'It Makes Me Sick.' You heard that, didn't you? You were there then. But I didn't. Play it or throw up. Yuri asked for it too, because he wanted me to do it because he asked. He wanted me to play it for him, but he wanted to be sure I wouldn't, not even for him. I didn't. Or I wouldn't. I played all of the *Dreams*, and they danced. Yuri danced, and girls danced with him, and everybody danced. They knew why I was there. They knew what I wanted. Finally, I could sense it, they were willing to give him up."

"What went wrong?"

"I don't know, except they weren't willing, not to give him up. It was so dark I couldn't see anything clearly. Yuri was in a corner, with these girls all over him, but that wasn't what he wanted. I am what he wanted, that's not it. He said he should have known they would do something to the cake, he shouldn't have taken the piece. He said he knew now he couldn't get rid of it, he would always know he might fall back into it again. He would always never be sure he wouldn't. He said he couldn't stand living that way. Without any faith in himself.

"I couldn't give him that. I could only give him my

faith in him, and that wasn't enough. He had to give himself faith too.

"Because he almost did come with me. He got up, stood up, away from those girls—and they were hanging on to him, everybody was hanging on to him, sort of, or hanging off one another, like a human chain. Yuri said he'd come home with me and they were holding him back at the same time that they were telling him to go for it, he'd be fine, he'd be happy, he was one lucky guy.

"And we almost made it.

"We got about halfway down the hall, and it was hard because they couldn't let him go. It was up to Yuri. I was holding his hand. I was holding Yuri's hand," she said, and slipped into silence, remembering.

I kept silent too.

"Somebody called from behind us, from in the living room. Called out, 'It hurts, man. You know how bad it hurts.'

"Yuri turned around and went back in.

"He pulled his hand free, as if I were holding him against his will, and then he stopped still. Looking at me for a minute. Before he went back down the hall, back into the living room.

"Only Yuri could have done it, for himself, and he didn't. Or he wouldn't. Or he couldn't.

"Somebody tells him that it hurts, and what could I say, Enny?"

I didn't know.

"I could feel him leaving me. I turned to him, without

any song to sing. He turned away from me. He went back down the hallway. What kind of fools are they if they think life is never going to hurt? If they think they can be safe and never hurt and still be alive? Can you imagine it?" Orfe asked.

"Yes," I said.